ALIBI FOR A DEAD MAN
A Bug and Roche Mystery

You'd think robbing a bank would be an easy way to make money. Outside of the occasional shot fired at you, a bank is where the money exists, and is yours for the having. While this idea may be okay for the casual robber, it doesn't hold true for the professional. If you want the bucks, but don't want to get shot or do time in the nearest pen, then robbing banks is very hard.

The best way to rob a bank is to be there when other people ain't and to leisurely load the dough into the handy bag you brought for the occasion. To be there when people ain't means a lot of planning, cause there are often people there, people with guns. So, if you want to make a living on other people's money then don't ever, and I mean ever, rob a bank during banker's hours, or even during waking hours. Rob a bank at night…

ALIBI FOR A DEAD MAN
BY WILSON TONEY

Stark House Press • Eureka California

ALIBI FOR A DEAD MAN

Published by Stark House Press
1315 H Street
Eureka, CA 95501, USA
griffinskye3@sbcglobal.net
www.starkhousepress.com

ALIBI FOR A DEAD MAN copyright © 2019 by Wilson Toney. All rights reserved, including the right of reproduction in whole or in part in any form. Published by Stark House Press by arrangement with the author and Brio Books.

ISBN-13: 978-1-944520-86-1

Book text and cover design by Jeff Vorzimmer, ¡calientedesign, Austin, Texas

PUBLISHER'S NOTE:
This is a work of fiction. Names, characters, places and incidents are either the products of the author's imagination or used fictionally, and any resemblance to actual persons, living or dead, events or locales, is entirely coincidental. Without limiting the rights under copyright reserved above, no part of this publication may be reproduced, stored, or introduced into a retrieval system or transmitted in any form or by any means (electronic, mechanical, photocopying, recording or otherwise) without the prior written permission of both the copyright owner and the above publisher of the book.

First Stark House Press Edition: December 2019

To Robin for forty some odd years of putting up with me, to Jason and Lee for being my proudest accomplishments and to Greg Shepard for giving me a chance.

ALPHA—THE MYSTERY BEGINS

You often hear that we are all star stuff. People should know the truth. What happens is that a star explodes at the end of its life and the atoms that make humans come from that explosion. We are not star stuff. We are star vomit. That explains a lot about the human condition.

—The wisdom (or lack thereof) of Bug

THE PUZZLE PALACE

There's a building in an unnamed town that is not any more noticeable than any other building in any other town. It does have bulletproof glass and blast-resistant walls but then so do many others (perhaps not with as much reason as this building). Other than these refinements, there isn't anything that makes this building stand out. Which is precisely what its denizens desire.

The building houses the personnel of the National Detective Agency for this city and that is reason enough for bulletproof glass and blast-resistant walls. The employees of this agency make many enemies and very few friends. Fortunately, they make lots of money and the company, which has been in business for over a century, thinks the profits are a fair trade-off for the building modifications required to keep someone on the wrong end of one of their investigation from doing too much damage when they try to settle the score with the odd drive-by shooting.

There are agents in this building, mostly middle-aged, experienced people that are doing their best at a thankless job, but doing it to the best of their ability and better than some and worse than others. While National has employees of all ages, colours, creeds and sexes, through the luck of the draw the agents involved in this particular story are three middle-aged men who are quite skilled, but also quite jaded. They'd rather have an easy job as a hard job, but easy or hard, it is their job and they will do their best, because that's what they are paid to do.

They like that pay, by the way.

NO EASY MONEY

You'd think robbing a bank would be an easy way to make money. Outside of the occasional shot fired at you, a bank is where the money exists, and is yours for the having. While this idea may be okay for the casual robber—the high school dropout, too lazy to work and too scared to sell drugs like an honest man—it doesn't hold true for the professional. If you want the bucks, but don't want to get shot or do time in the nearest pen, then robbing banks is very hard.

The best way to rob a bank is to be there when other people ain't and to leisurely load the dough into the handy bag you brought for the occasion. To be there when people ain't means a lot of planning, cause there are often people there, people with guns and people that can send out a signal to the cops with just a slight push of a well-concealed button. So, if you want to make a living on other people's money then don't ever, and I mean ever, rob a bank during banker's hours, or even during waking hours. Rob a bank at night, when the money is in the vault and armed guards aren't likely to take a random potshot in your direction.

For some reason, banks keep their vaults well protected with all sorts of electronic gizmos and random checks by security guards and even nightly patrols by the cops. This is irksome for the bank robbing professional, since it means a lot of nights of watching a bank to get the routine of the bank security professionals, which can be obtained of course, since humans are creatures of habits. A random check usually happens between say 1 and 3 a.m. and the cops always come around 3.30 a.m. Thus, if you come late, you can expect to have good luck between 4 a.m. and

6 a.m. (gotta get out by 6 a.m. as that's when the custodial staff enters the premises for the day).

Something else that is out of your control, but can become part of your planning, is the weather. A rainy day, particularly a downpour, will lessen the zeal of the looker-outers for the bank, and the random patrol will definitely not be during the downpour. The cops will, at most, just whiz by and make sure there are no unaccounted-for cars in the parking lot. This set of circumstances—heavy rain, a crook who knows electronics, a crook who knows vaults, a crook who's the interior lookout and strong arm in case it's needed, and a driver who won't bolt just because he saw something from the corner of his eye—means the possibility of successfully pulling off a bank heist is enhanced though not guaranteed. Nothing in life is guaranteed.

One more thing that has to be available, that is, if you've been at the game for a while and your proclivities are known by the local constabulary, the thing that is critical, and the thing that is hardest but still doable, is to have an alibi. "But officer, I couldn't have possibly done the deed as I was at the First Church of all true believers at the time" doesn't usually work, as the cops can easily check whether the First Church was open at the time and whether anyone was there and if they were did they remember you. No, a more sophisticated alibi is needed. What's more important is the alibi must be checkable and easily proven, because that will mean the cops won't even bother you, as they have their proof that you couldn't be there because you were proven to be elsewhere. And not by your lying brother-in-law, but by some system that you couldn't rig ahead of time. Unless you could rig the system ahead of time, of course.

Everything was set: the forecast for heavy rain, the bank schedules for both the rent-a-cops and the local fuzz, the rigged alibi, with the date locked in and selected just because of that forecast of rain. All that was left was to do the deed.

And that is precisely what this band of brothers had done. On the fifteenth of a certain night they were engaged at a bar, in a back room, playing poker, but under surveillance by the video system. They were also robbing a local bank of approximately $4 million dollars. This would have made them very happy except that their ace driver, driving through the rain which really was coming down, was sideswiped by another guy who was driving on this Godforsaken night and the two cars rolled, killing the driver of the other car and also killing Randolph Butree, the electronics guy, who was now dead when he had to be playing poker. This wouldn't do, of course, for a man can't be dead on one side of town and playing poker on the other side at the same time. So the surviving thieves had to come up with another plan in order to preserve the alibi since the bank had already been robbed and they sure as hell weren't gonna take the loot back. Their spontaneous plan, though not ingenious, was the best they could do given the circumstances.

CHASER

Joel Cready was listening on the police scanner and watching the twitter feed of several cops that he knew and who knew him but would likely not want to admit it. The email was open and he was sitting in his car awaiting any news of car accidents, or work accidents, or any other sort of mayhem that might require the services of a true professional in law who made a buck by getting clients for his lawyers and a payment of five to ten grand.

Cready considered himself a man of compassion. Upon learning of an accident, he would head to the scene and have a steaming cup of coffee available for the injured, and blankets if need be, and a kind word, and the name and address of the law firm that employed him to chase down potential clients for their lawsuits against the man. Or the woman for that matter, as they were not sexist but an equal opportunity suer and glad to sue anyone for anything if they could get their 40 per cent.

Now Cready couldn't just swoop down on the potential client without some pretence, so he would often say, "Just happened by and I saw the commotion, let me help, please. The least a fellow can do, have a cup of coffee … think nothing of it, happy to help my fellow man. By the way, I was in an awful accident about three years ago, I got legal representation, but good. Let me tell you, these guys at Feinstein and Gray made me a mint. Matter of fact I think they'd be more than happy to help you. Wait a minute, I think I got a card here. Dogged if I don't. Call them or, better yet, why don't you give me your name and number and I'll have someone call you? I don't mind calling them for you. Least I could do."

To work his charade, Cready had to be on good terms with the cops who were often at the scene either ahead or sometimes behind him. Cops, being human, would upset his game by telling the potential suckers, that is clients, that Cready would get money for his humanitarian effort and thus muddy the waters. So Cready developed his police pals the same as most people do—by giving them money under the table, or by going by their bars and buying them drinks and laughing at their corny jokes and treating them as other humans (which sometimes was sufficient as cops don't get treated as humans all that often).

As a result of all this glad handing, buying drinks and the occasional under the table tip as Cready referred to it, he came to know a lot of cops and they came to know him. They also knew if they tipped him to a likely accident, there was a quick hundred in it for them, regardless of whether he got his sucker, er that is client, under the wing of Feinstein and Gray.

This practice of getting tips from the cops was illegal as hell, but if the cop had a burner phone, and most did, then unless the phone was found on them during an inspection of some sort, then there wasn't any way of tracing calls from them to Cready.

On the night of the fifteenth, Cready was called by an Officer McNabb. "Got a live one," said a voice that Cready recognised immediately. "Higgins Lane, the last mailbox I saw said 1417. Car accident. Looks like two dead, and one is holding a towel I gave him against his forehead and it's bloody. Don't know if he's the driver or at fault but he may be neither or both. Don't shout if it's a wasted trip."

"I never do," Cready said truthfully. He hung up and plugged in the address. Immediately he started in the direction of Higgins Lane. A small place in a big city, but really a country lane as it was on the outskirts. Cready was smiling, as he had a potential ten grand in his sights. He wouldn't smile for long however.

THE INSECTS

Bug and I had just finished our trip down south, which was lucrative and more fun than taking girly pictures, but that's neither here nor there. A man takes his job as he finds it and believe me, seeing and photographing half-naked women ain't all it's cracked up to be.

So Bug and I were available as they say, and the dispatcher knew it and the jerk passed the info along to Thompson who's not the best boss in the world, but not the worst either. As I was having my second cup of really bad Joe—office coffee—and skimming the web for something good to read, my phone rings and the dispatcher says, "Thompson wants you and Bug right away."

"Got it," was all I was up to saying since my repartee ain't at its best at 8.30 of a morning after a late flight that hadn't gotten me home until after midnight.

Bug was sitting at his desk, which was right next to mine, in the bullpen, which is what we called the wide open area where we had our cubicles, if you could call them that. A desk, a phone, a partition on the front and to either side, but the partitions were only about shoulder high so you could still see a lot, and you could hear everything. That feature has its drawbacks for would-be Romeos, but after a while you just ignore the ambient sound unless your name is called, so I said loudly, "Bug, Thompson wants us."

"Gonna give us a bonus, no doubt," Bug said as he pushed back his chair and stood up, "after the way we solved the Tillerman case."

"As I recall, we didn't solve squat, but we were told the truth by one of the perps right before he died from some damn drug he took. More likely he wants to guide us on what not to put on our travel voucher."

"That's all right," Bug said. "I got enough stuff on mine that even if he throws out half, I'll make out okay."

I half-laughed, mostly cause I knew it to be true, as Bug was one of the most imaginative fellows I ever knew when it came to filling out a travel voucher.

We walked the forty-two steps down from my cube to Thompson's office together, giving the dispatcher the evil eye for doing his job, and he gladly returned it to us. Thompson was just hanging up his phone when we walked in. He smiled at us and said, "My favourite insects."

My name is David Roche, which is supposed to be pronounced Rock but always comes out as Roch-ee or Roach by those who don't know me that well. Thompson knew me very well but it was his favourite joke to call us the insects, since Bug was a nickname, though I never understood how John Wallis could be translated into Bug. Still, Bug and Roche were partners and we were called the insects around this house of laughter.

I smiled weakly, since I cared about my next evaluation. Bug just stood there solemn, as he didn't care about much of anything and particularly not his next evaluation.

"I heard your trip to the sunny south came out about as well as could be expected," Thompson said in his booming voice, and then he laughed, though if there was any humour in what he said it was beyond me.

"Yeah," was my brilliant reply.

"Well, that's alright then. Pull up the chairs as I have another real case for you." That meant non-divorce type work, which we really didn't expect, seeing as how most of what we do is take pictures of philanderers or try to find hidden assets. To me it was as real as any other work, but for some reason the higher ups thought less of it. I didn't know why, cause it definitely kept the lights on at this joint.

"We have been retained by Feinstein and Gray on a car accident," Thompson said. "But it's unusual in one respect. The person who was in the accident wants us to prove that he was not at fault, which stands to reason, but even if we prove it, he would not likely get any money, since he wasn't badly injured, and the guy who hit him doesn't seem to have any assets."

That was unusual. I'd worked several of these accident cases and typically we were trying to dig dirt on one side in order to get to their personal assets. If it's just the insurance involved, it rarely goes to trial, since the insurance company will likely settle up to the maximum of the coverage if need be, and will settle for less if they can. But you're generally talking a quarter to a half million at most, which is a lot of beans to the average joe, but chump change to the insurance company. They'll put up with some hassle and some legal expenses but not a lot, and lawyers know this and generally settle out of court, which makes them richer but may not be the best for their client.

"There's a kicker," Thompson went on then took a sip of a fancy coffee he had brought in with him when he showed up late for work, as he often did. No office coffee for the gentry, leave that for the riff raff. "The guy involved in the accident was an independent contractor of theirs, a guy named Cready who I'm sure you guys already know. He's one of their chasers."

"Yeah," Bug said in a monotone. "Everybody knows Cready."

I nodded that I too had the misfortune to know Joel Cready. He was an A1 ambulance chaser who made more money in a year than I would in three, and he was also a nuisance and would try to muddy up any case that happened to fall under the Feinstein and Gray umbrella. He was often an expert witness, since he was at the accident site prior to any of us lowly investigators, and his memory of what happened, or at least what he said happened, correlated remarkably well with the interests of Feinstein and Gray.

"So Cready was involved in an accident," I said. "That's likely an occupational hazard, since his duty is to chase ambulances and such, which often requires a bit more speed than the limit allows. And I've seen him drive—he often has a phone stuck to his ear, or else is checking his email as he flits about. Doesn't surprise me that he was in an accident. It does surprise me that this law firm, Frankenstein and whatits, gives a damn. There are other chasers they can obtain."

"Quite true, David," Thompson said. "There are likely other factors that we are not privy to, because I've worked with Feinstein and Gray before and they generally aren't interested in anything unless there's a buck in it for them. Not much pro bono from that firm. Likely Cready has them over a barrel, but that's not our concern. Our job is to see if there is something to Mr Cready's claim that the other car was driving without headlights and whether the other driver, a Mr Butree, has a history that includes copious amounts of drink or illicit drugs."

Thompson pulled out the preliminary report from a messy file of folders on his desk and tossed it to me. "Read at your desk, then have Bug read. All the particulars are in the report. The short version is this: Cready received a call at about 1 a.m. on the fifteenth, just last week, from an anonymous source—which probably means a cop on the dole—that there was an accident out at Higgins Lane and that an enterprising chaser might make a buck if he got there toot sweet. So Cready hauls it towards this accident and up at Lancaster he T-bones a car that he said was driving without headlights and ran a stop sign. Mr Butree—by the way I've got skip trace already working on his background—is DOA. Cready's shaken a bit, but not a whole lot. His biggest care seems to be that he'd miss out on the bucks he could have made as a chaser up at Higgins.

"A couple of cops show up, cause Cready phoned the accident in, and likely others had phoned it in also as the accident was blocking the road." Thompson's short version didn't seem that short in the listening. "The cops look the accident scene over, smell Cready's breath, which, and he will admit to this, contained some alcohol, but even if it was under the legal limit which he claimed, was still a bad sign. They didn't see any skid marks for Cready's car, and Cready said there wouldn't be any as the guy was running without his lights on. This has not yet been proved, but the cops are trying to see if it's true. They seem to think Cready was a bit impaired and was thinking this might be vehicular homicide or some such."

Thompson shrugged his shoulders. "Cops, God bless 'em, without their suspicious minds we wouldn't get half the work we get. At any rate, they thought the whole situation was fishy, and to top it off, they find there's no accident up at Higgins, thus it made them suspicious of the rest of Cready's story. This morning, Feinstein and Gray contacted our firm and we signed a contract for a maximum of two weeks effort for two men. You fortunate gentlemen were available and thus we selected you to find the truth."

"And if the truth ain't to their liking?" Bug asked.

"We'll cross that Rubicon when necessary," Thompson said. "Hopefully we'll find that Mr Butree was a raging alcoholic, fresh from a bar just off Lancaster and footage from the ever-present security camera shows him staggering off just before the accident."

"Given our luck," Bug said, "we'll find he's a Baptist minister that never touched a drop in his life."

"Well," Thompson sighed, "you will find what you will find. If we can twist it for the benefit of our client we will. If it's black and white that Cready is at fault, then that's his lookout. I leave the finding in your capable hands."

We both nodded and turned to leave.

"Don't be too overly creative on your travel vouchers from your southern trip," Thompson added. "I'll be looking at them very closely, and that goes double for you, Bug."

"Why, I'm the most honest man in the National Detective Agency," Bug lied.

MALARKEY FOR STARKEY

Joe Starkey walked into the home office of United Transhipment, which meant he was walking into a very foreign place. Joe was used to beer and baseball and bought babes, and this was the home of wine and soccer and ... well higher priced bought babes.

What exactly the bright people at United Transhipment did in the world of business wasn't clear to Starkey, but whatever it was, it paid a hell of a lot more than the private investigation racket. The building where this firm resided was in the middle of downtown, which had the highest land value in the city and probably the whole state. The interior of the building was only the finest woods and fancy stains on said wood. Even the receptionist was beautiful and likely made more for directing people to the bowels of the building (if a building as ornate as this was crude enough to have bowels) than Starkey made for his twenty years of skills in his racket.

The lithesome lady, with almost ash-blonde hair and what seemed like a designer's dress, looked at Joe with just a hint of disapproval—Joe's idea of high fashion was whatever was on sale at Wal-Mart while he happened to be picking up beer—before directing him to the office of Mr Jack Nebo Esquire. She had first phoned Mr Nebo's secretary to make sure that this, er gentleman, was expected and had an appointment to get into the promised land. But once past the lovely but efficient and just a bit condescending lady, Starkey found his way easily enough to Nebo's office on the third floor.

The office itself was plush and ornate, with a crew of four people who looked like normal if well-dressed people sitting in a front room as if protecting the bigger room at the back. One of the four looked up as

Starkey entered, a young man who appeared to be fresh out of college, and came over to the door. The other three didn't even glance up, which meant either there were a lot of people that came into these offices or else Starkey really didn't have movie star looks as he always assumed. The young man extended his hand and said, "Welcome, Mr Starkey, Mr Nebo is awaiting you in his office."

Starkey shook the extended hand and followed the young man as he headed towards the office at the back of the room. The young man knocked once, then opened the door and said, "Mr Starkey, sir." The man then held the door open and let Starkey through.

Starkey entered the even more plush and exquisitely detailed inner office. The decorations that were placed, without doubt though Starkey wouldn't know from his studies on the matter, just right to show the contrived ambiance of good taste, cost more than a pretty penny. In addition to the requisite degrees and placards showing all of the colleges and certifications that Mr Nebo had obtained in his illustrious careers, there were lots of original paintings from more than likely famous artists that Starkey had never heard of.

Mr Nebo was a very slim man, and Starkey had now seen six people at the firm and all had been very slim, which either meant the place ruined their digestion or else it was required in order to hang onto a highly coveted position. Nebo was past fifty, wearing a very nice suit that Starkey thought looked uncomfortable for work, but just right to project an air of genteel wealth. He smiled and extended his hand.

"Thanks for coming down, Mr Starkey," Nebo said and jerked his head towards a comfortable chair at the front of his desk. "Have a chair and let's talk."

"It's why I'm here," Starkey admitted.

"I don't know if your firm told you," Nebo said, "that I requested you personally, but I did. You were recommended to me by my doctor of all people."

Starkey smiled and nodded. He did know he had been requested by name but he figured it had to be something like that or National would have sent a more senior guy, or probably a couple of senior guys. This place looked like it could provide a buck or two towards the bottom line, and National always tried to impress those with a buck or two, or fifty thousand, that they could obtain for their services.

"My doctor had the misfortune, as he states it, to meet you during a case that you involved him in quite recently," Nebo continued. "He said that you understood financial dealings and that he found you annoying as hell, but honourable. It was the annoying as hell part that made me want to have you work on our behalf."

Starkey grinned at that, maybe this guy was gonna be all right after all.

"We have a situation," Nebo said. "One of our senior men, a Mr Chuck Garson, has not come into work for the past three days. Mr Garson has not been seen by anyone, not even the fellow tenants of his building where he resides as best we can determine. We wish to employ the National Detective Agency in general, and you in particular, to find Mr Garson."

"Gone to the cops yet?" Starkey asked. Assuming the answer was no, since this was sizing up as a case of some sort of swindle or ethically challenged stock deal, he was surprised with the answer.

"Oh yes," Nebo said with a nod of his stylishly greying hair. "We called on the second day that Mr Garson was missing. They were the ones who told us no one in the building where he lived had seen him for the past few days."

"I'm not trying to turn the work down," Starkey said but only half meant it, since he would rather be doing something easier like chasing after cheating husbands with a camera rather than missing business men. "But I don't know we can do anything the cops can't do, and they don't cost you a cent."

"What is free often has opportunity costs not seen by the unschooled," Nebo answered, which meant squat to Starkey and the blankness on his face must have shown. Nebo continued, "What I meant was there is always a trade off in everything we do, and while it's true the police will give the case their due diligence, they won't be actively involved as one who is doing it for money. We need Mr Garson to be found and we need, more importantly, information that Mr Garson has found. The police might find Mr Garson and after talking with him, may decide that we don't need to know of his whereabouts. You, however, will be in our employ and thus will be glad to tell us his whereabouts, or the whereabouts of the information we seek."

"Okay," Starkey said. "If you're willing to pay our rates, we will be more than willing to work for you. Just one thing for you to note, and no insult is meant by what I am about to say as I say it to all my clients, if we find Garson and this information and it looks like whatever we find is legally questionable in any way, shape of form, we take it to the cops. We have no desire to be any higher on their crap list than we already are."

"Do as you think best in that regard," Nebo answered. "Mr Garson is one of our best people at overseas financial transactions. Some of these transactions involve strict banking accounting procedures where only the correct set of numbers are required to obtain the monies therein. We have reason to believe that Mr Garson has not been on the straight and narrow when it comes to dealing with some of our clients' funds, and we need those banking codes in order to check on that issue."

Starkey nodded. "So Garson has transferred funds from clients into his own account and you need the Swiss bank passwords to get it back. Of course, you don't want publicity on this, since your clients may not have gotten wind of it yet and will likely scream to the feds when they do, and United Transhipment will be out the money to give them back their lost funds as well as the bad publicity, which will cause even greater losses."

"That is succinct and correct," Nebo said. "Our clientele are people that have often obtained money in unorthodox ways, and they use our services to ensure the money is put into a safe place where they can be certain that it is safe. They don't care about anything except the safety of their money, and will pay us a carrying fee as well as a service fee in order to ensure that safety."

"You launder their money," Starkey said flatly.

"Not at all," Nebo replied. "Though it is likely we get the money after it has been laundered. We are audited often, and we do internal audits very often ourselves to make sure we are not laundering money. But even if you follow all financial rules there is still some room for judgement, and let me say, that we judge to do things that are in the best interest of our clients and not necessarily the best interest of the IRS."

"If you are playing with the types of clients that you say, then there may be a high possibility that Garson was kidnapped for those bank passwords. It seems to me, if I understand how this works, there are no questions asked by the bankers as long as you have the code. Which means Garson may already be dead and the money long gone."

"That is true," Nebo said. "But we still need to find that truth, if possible before the next quarterly report is released, which will happen in about a month. The clients affected will see that their bank funds have decreased and they will suspect our firm of having a hand in it. We are not, of course, supposed to know their personal codes, but we often do, since it allows us to do a lot of the work without having to bother them."

"Okay," Starkey said, "I will be glad to look into it. I will first need a contract and I would like for you to let the police know personally that your firm is hiring us. They won't mind, since they don't like to do missing persons work all that much anyway, and we typically get along on these types of cases, but as I said before, if something looks dicey, National will take it to the cops. We have to work with them daily and we try, sometimes with very little success, to not irritate them."

"Again," Nebo replied, "use your judgement on legal issues. We will have the contracts in place by this afternoon. We would like daily reports, even if nothing has been found."

"My bosses will get the daily report," Starkey assured Nebo, "and I think they'll be glad to submit them to you, but it's their call and not mine, so you may want to put that into the contract. You can call me at any time and I'll tell you whatever I think I can. But I do have bosses and I work for National not you. If you can't live with that, you might want to hire someone that can work only for you."

"I'm sure we will work out the details," Nebo replied. "National has a good name and has many more rich and varied resources than a lone investigator would have. We will ask for the daily report in our contract and negotiate agreeable terms."

Starkey smiled as he arose to leave. "You make the money good enough and I assure you the terms will be agreeable. Please send a list of any known associates as well as Garson's phone numbers, email and address. Thanks for your time and thanks for the work. I hope we can be of service."

FUZZY HILL

After reading the report on Cready, which was at best sketchy, Bug and I grabbed a company car and headed out to Lancaster to see the accident site. We had been to many accident scenes in our career, for we were often hired to dig dirt when a lawsuit was being threatened. You sometimes, maybe even often, find stuff the cops overlooked. It's not that they're bad at their jobs, but they're busy just like the rest of us, and when you're busy you miss things. I once found a liquor bottle that a culprit had tossed just by going through the bushes ten feet away from the wreckage. The cops should have found it and would have usually but not this time. This time the cops had missed it. That was why I always visited the site, even when it was several days later.

Bug had dialled up Cready and asked him to meet us there and Cready had readily agreed. I wasn't sure I wanted him to meet us there, since he might influence us in some way, but you never know, so we decided to invite him and get his take on the wreck while we checked out the site.

Cready was waiting as we pulled up to the wrecked site at Lancaster. "Go up Fuzzy Hill Road," he told us as we rolled down our window and he pointed to a steep hill that had a stop sign at the end of the road. "About halfway up, there's a house on the left with an extra-long curved driveway, the owner gave me his permission for us to park there."

We followed his instructions and found the long curved driveway. We parked as politely as possible, making sure that any other cars that entered the driveway could get by, but not parking too far on the grass. As we got out to walk back down to the site Bug said, "Dollars to donuts Cready has been here more than once or else he wouldn't know about this place or have permission from the owner."

"Meaning?" I asked.

"Meaning," Bug replied, "Cready's a trained investigator, just like you and me, he knows what can pull his butt out of the fire, and he's had time to salt the site with various and sundry things he has concocted."

"You're too pessimistic, Bug," I said.

"You want to know the difference between wisdom and pessimism?"

"What?"

"Not a damn thing."

I half-snorted because I had set myself up for that one, then we were too busy walking down the steep Fuzzy Hill Road. It was beautiful but deadly—like a lot of women I wish I had known in my time, and the ones that Bug insists he has known—a very steep road that came to an abrupt end at the intersection with Lancaster. It was however, greener than Ireland and it was meticulously mowed, including the steep sides of the hills. Somebody earned their money with that mowing.

It took us a good five minutes to walk down the hill, and I swear it was about as hard coming down and fighting the gravity in the descent as it was to climb up and fight the gravity on the ascent. Once we finally got to the bottom, I turned and looked back up the hill, and with one glance I knew this wasn't the first accident at this location. The civil engineer that designed this intersection should have been forced to live there.

Cready was pacing about on the side of the road, keeping a lookout for the light traffic that was about at this early part of the morning. This was a residential district and it would be busy in the morning and in the afternoon, but other than that, likely not so much. It was a good half-hour with non-rush traffic to get here from our office which was near downtown, so I didn't see that there would be many people that lived here were gonna come home for lunch.

Cready reached out and shook my hand and then Bug's and said, "Glad you guys are here and on my side. Heaven knows I'm gonna need it."

"Not if what you said was true," I replied. "Care to tell us, in your own words, what happened?"

"Glad to," Cready said. "I was coming up Lancaster from the city," he pointed his finger towards the way we had just driven, "I was speeding a bit, but I won't admit that in court of course, and just as I swung around that curve a car comes flying out of Fuzzy Hill Road. If I had been five seconds sooner or later it would have missed me and ran into the ditch on that side of Lancaster," and again he motioned with his hand, though he didn't need to as it was evident where a car coming down Fuzzy Hill would have to wind up.

Cready continued with his story. "The car had no headlights on, there was no sound of horn and no brakes squealing, it was just two objects occupying the same space at the same time and boom, I T-bone the other car, which is bad but would have been worse for me if it had T-boned me, so I ain't complaining on that score. I jump out of the car and run over to help the guy out of the car. He was dead, you could tell. I also felt him, and he was cold. I repeat, he was cold."

"That," said Bug in all his wisdom and twenty years of experience, "puts a different twist on the whole shebang."

"We haven't seen the police report yet, but if what you said is true, it should be your salvation," I said. "He would have had to have been dead for a while to feel cold, and obviously the wreck couldn't have killed him. Why did you need us?"

"The cops took their sweet time getting here," Cready answered and grinned. "Just my luck, they're always johnnie on the spot and ready to spoil my game at most accidents, unless I grease them of course, but for me, they took well over four hours. They have their reasons, not the least of which is they ain't got time and they ain't got people and there were forty zillion other things nagging at them."

"It usually takes about twelve hours for a body to cool, given only four hours they still should have felt the difference," Bug said.

Creasy replied, "Well, the police felt the body and it was cool, but after four hours, on a windy night, that didn't surprise them. Also, the forensic team never did show up, after all this was a car accident, not a shooting. By the time they got the body back to the lab, it would have already cooled naturally. So that's part of the reason I'm in the soup."

"Only part?" I asked.

Cready rolled his eyes and squinted back up the hill, then he pointed at the very top and said, "You let a car go from up there and it will be doing at least 40 mph by the time it hits this spot. Let's say I've timed it a couple of times with another car, and just break before I get to the intersection to keep from going into the ditch. It wouldn't take a genius to figure out when to release the car, given you've seen the headlights of another car just coming over the hump, down at Lancaster," he again pointed with his finger. We couldn't see the hump because of the curve, but we had witnessed it first hand on our drive up.

"You've checked that you can see a car on the hump from the top of Fuzzy Hill?" Bug asked.

"Oh yeah," Cready said. "You'd be surprised how your investigative skills sharpen when your neck's on the line, but I want you to check it out too. Never take a guy's word unless you check, investigation one oh one."

"We will," I replied and we would because we too knew to never take a guy's word for anything, and that especially included a chaser who lied for a living and thus got very good at it.

"Still," Bug said with the doubt very evident in his voice, "a lot of luck would still be required, you would have to be up at the top of the hill, just at the right moment, see car lights coming, release at the right time, hope the car's speed coming up Lancaster didn't change a whole lot, hope nobody saw you waiting at the top of the hill to release the car, hope you weren't seen during the trial runs ... That's a lot to hope for."

"I didn't say it was the best plan and sure proof," Cready said, "but it was what happened. Nothing else makes sense, cause the guy was dead before he was hit by my car. I'll stretch it even further: what if the guys knew when I'd be coming through here? That reduces the time they are on the top of Fuzzy Hill, plus it was two in the morning, so there weren't likely to be many people out and about anyway since this is mostly a working middle-class community. People are asleep. I say it figures, even if it was risky, it figures and it works for them."

I nodded at Cready, not that I agreed with him but I didn't want to shut him up, the more he talked the more we were likely to hear something that we liked.

"How were you set up?" I asked. "And more importantly, why were you set up?"

Cready shrugged his shoulders. "I think I can answer the how, but as to the why, you got me. Being a chaser, I don't make it on many Christmas card lists, as a lot of people I deal with put up with me only because they can make a buck off me. Well, I ain't in this racket because I want to be liked, the truth is, if you've got the gift of the gab and you don't mind long hours, you can make a very good living, and I do. So, I'm sure I've upset my rivals, and maybe a cop or two, but not enough they'd want to put me in the slammer for vehicular manslaughter. As far as I know no one hates me that much, but with humans, you can never tell."

"If you can't give me the why, then at least the how," Bug jumped in before I could ask the same question.

"That's simple," Cready replied. "I hang out at a certain place in town, a parking lot near an all-night eatery, when I ain't busy and I wasn't that busy last night. Now, a lot of people, and especially a lot of cops, know I hang out here. All it would take would be for someone to call me about a car wreck in the right location, in this instance it was Higgins Lane, and a GPS to show the quickest way to Higgins Lane from there. That would result in my likely being on Lancaster at the right time for me to slam into the released car."

"So, as I understand it," I said, "you got a call from one of your sources and haul up here. Then you find out after that the call was faked. If that's true who was it from?"

"I can't say for sure but it sounded like Officer Paul McNabb," Creasy said. "The call was from a burner phone, which most of my calls are from. I got a copy of my phone numbers received from the cops and will circle the number for you, though I doubt it will do you a lot of good. A lot of cops buy burner phones every week or so, just to be on the safe side. They only cost fifteen bucks and well worth the investment if you are talking with people you don't want the shoo flies to know you're talking with."

"You got any reason to think McNabb has it in for you?" Bug asked Cready.

"Not anything I can think of," Cready replied. "Just another cop that I give a hundred to if he puts me onto something good. I've heard that he takes money from lots of others, and not just from chasers, but you hear that about a lot of cops. Most of them don't, but some do and that's a fact."

"We'll talk to him," I said. "Maybe if necessary, but not unless it's really necessary. Cops gather round during a storm and they resent anyone showing their dirt to the public. But we will keep an eye out as we investigate to see if there is a possible connection."

"I'll do some checking on my own," Cready said. "I don't mind any crap they throw my way, since it will still be a lot less crappy than going to stir for three to five."

"Do what you wish," Bug replied. "I don't blame you none either, but kindly keep our name out of it since we gotta work with the boys in blue and they ain't exactly friendly on their best day."

Cready was staring off into the distance and simply nodded to show he had heard what Bug had said. Bug and I said our goodbyes and walked back up Fuzzy Hill to our car. As we got to our car, panting and totally out of breath, Bug remarked, "You know, I gotta start getting to the gym if I hope to retain my girlish figure."

I nodded and knew what he meant, we both were models of physical perfection with only about eighty excess pounds of fat between us, with Bug having the greater share.

After we sat and rested as our blood pressure dropped and our breath became normal, I said, "Cready is either the best liar I ever knew or a very unlucky man. I go with the latter right now, but reserve the right to change my mind."

"Lots of ifs and buts and maybes," Bug replied. "Has to be right if he's being set up. I ain't no statistician, but you would think the probabilities wouldn't be in his favour."

"Yeah," I agreed. "But if you wanted to hide a dead body in plain sight, then this would be one way of doing it. Maybe not the best way, but one way, and if you were desperate enough, then you take the risks."

Bug just grunted, and I took that to mean the subject was talked out. It probably was. I cranked the car and we drove to the top of Fuzzy Hill. We verified Cready's statement that you could see a car coming over the hump and that once seen you could release a car with a dead man driving to crash into said car seen coming over the hump.

I put the car at the very top of Fuzzy Hill, put it in neutral and rolled down. I slammed on the brakes towards the bottom to keep from rolling past the stop sign and into the intersection. We had hit 40 mph on our descent and it took about five seconds.

Cready was still standing on the side of the road, looking up and down the hill, and towards the curve and back. He smiled when he saw our car coming towards him. The fact that we were trying to see if we could duplicate the supposed conditions didn't seem to bother him.

After the car screamed to a stop, I noted the information on a small pad that I kept on me for that purpose, for no other reason than it's what an investigator does. Then I turned the car back on Lancaster and waved at Cready.

Cready just nodded and went right back to looking up and down Fuzzy Hill. I didn't understand why it held such fascination for him, but then again, I wasn't the one looking at three to five in the joint. We headed towards the cops to get a copy of the report. I didn't look forward to it, as I never look forward to talking to cops. Call it prejudice, if you wish, but I think it's wisdom.

THE LAMEST GUY

"This building is immaculate," Starkey told the superintendent of the Hobart Arms. He didn't mean it, even if it was true.

"Don't need no compliments," the superintendent said. "Just pony up the fifty and I'll open the door. Otherwise, keep on blowing hard, just don't blow hard around here."

The superintendent was fiftyish, had been around more than one investigator and knew that the going rate for accidentally leaving the door open on an apartment of interest was fifty bucks. Since he was not exactly in the one per cent being the super of a building—even a nice building such as this one—the extra fifty would help come the end of month when the liquor bill rolled in.

Starkey pulled his wallet out and counted two twenties and a ten and said, "I don't doubt that the residents overflow your bank account at Christmas."

"You'd think that, wouldn't you, but the cheap bastards must be Hindu or something cause they sure don't send anything my way at Christmas or any other time." If there was an insult in Starkey's line, and there was, then it went right over his head.

Finally, the superintendent opened the door to Chuck Garson's apartment, after first looking at the two twenties and ten for a second and then holding them up to the light to make sure he saw the security strip. He didn't want any counterfeit, and doubtless Starkey looked like a guy who'd pass a counterfeit buck to save himself a real buck. While that was true, Starkey was playing with company money here and the money was genuine US currency, probably chock full of cocaine.

"Knock on my door when you leave," the superintendent said, "so I'll know to come back up and lock up. Don't steal nothing, either."

Starkey nodded, then slipped by the Superintendent into the apartment. It was spacious, sparse and not overly well kept with clothes still on the floor of the living room. There were no pictures on the walls, no portraits, no family shots or even a simple picture of a man and woman together. It looked like what it was—a bachelor pad.

Starkey went through the place with minimal impact. He wasn't looking for anything in particular, just looking, and sometimes when you are just looking you find something worth looking for. This was one of those cases.

There was a pad of paper that was sitting right beside the phone. The pad had several phone numbers written on it. Starkey took a picture and would send it to skip trace for their help. More than likely they were burner phones if there was anything nefarious going on. Crooks and drug dealers kept the burner phone industry in business.

Starkey went into the bedroom and looked over the unmade bed. The closet held a lot of fancy clothes, which showed that even if Garson was a messy housekeeper he was immaculate when he dressed. At least when he dressed for work, as there were also some beat-up old blue jeans and a sweater that had the name of some obscure college that Starkey had never heard of. He wrote the name down on his pad just in case.

Starkey gently went through the clothing drawers and found nothing except underwear, socks and way too many ties. Doubtless the guy had to wear a different tie for every day of the month and doubtless he could with the selection Starkey found.

Starkey poked around in the bathroom, found some prescription medicines that might lead to something; there was a Xanax bottle and a couple of other prescription meds that might indicate that Garson was battling depression. It could also just mean that Garson liked the feel he got from those drugs and was faking depression to obtain them, but Starkey wrote down the name of the drugs and the name of the doctor that prescribed them.

Starkey checked carefully behind the sink and toilet in the bathroom as well as inside the cistern. Those were favourite places to hide things you didn't want the neighbours to see, but he found nothing, not even some weed which he half expected.

Finally, he had looked through everyplace except the one place where people always hid stuff in an apartment. You see, an apartment, especially a three-room apartment, ain't all that big to begin with, and it's laid out to maximise the utility. That meant there were very few places that you could really hide something you didn't want anyone to find. But there was always an air vent, and everyone seemed to think that something hidden in an air vent was as safe as if it was in Fort Knox.

Starkey pulled up a chair to stand on, and then pulled out his swiss knife that he and most other investigators carried, cause you always check the air vent when you search an apartment. He noted right away that the screws were bright and shiny, which indicated that the vent had been used, probably often and recently, since most screws become dull in a very short time when they're not used. Given his judgement of the superintendent, Starkey didn't think the guy was the type that worried about ensuring the screws were bright or dull, so that meant Garson had bought his own screws and put them into the vent holder, and recently.

It took only a minute to unscrew the vent plate, because the screws definitely had not had time to freeze in the plate. Sure enough there was a small brown envelope in the vent. Starkey withdrew it and stepped off the chair to examine it.

The envelope contained three different identities and one key. The key was obviously meant for a safety deposit box. The identities were likely meant for nefarious but enriching shenanigans that Mr Chuck Garson was a participant in.

Starkey smiled and said softly, "Gotcha."

Then he replaced the air vent plate and put the chair back where he found it. He made sure his shoe impressions did not show in the chair. Since he had worn gloves, he wasn't overly concerned with leaving any fingerprints behind, but to be sure he left no DNA evidence he wiped down everything visible with a towel he had brought for that purpose. The towel had been treated with an antibiotic that supposedly would erase or at least contaminate any DNA that was inadvertently left at the scene.

Starkey placed the towel back inside his coat, looked around the place one more time to make sure he hadn't missed anything, then walked out and quietly closed the door. He didn't bother to knock on the superintendent's door as he made his way quietly to the street.

SULLY THE KEEPER OF SECRETS

Bug had propped his feet up on Sully's desk which drew a growl from Sully. Bug smiled and put his feet back down. "Down right inhospitable in here, Sully."

"I wasn't raised in a barn," Sully replied. "And I don't particularly care to associate with them that were."

Bug said "Moo" which drew a smile from Sully but Bug kept his feet on the floor.

Bug and I were swapping lies and paying Sully for some previous work he had done for us, which made Sully happy. That was a mood that was highly atypical for Sully or any cop.

I had a copy of the police report on Cready's wreck and was gently trying to pump Sully for information without hitting the pay me button. It was delicate work. Sully, for all of his other charming qualities, wasn't a guy that gave an investigator squat for free.

"Any inside dope on this Cready wreck?" I asked. "Just between us brethren cops that is."

"You and I may have a relationship," Sully said, "but brethren ain't the right word for it. I prefer to consider it more like a cheapskate buyer and an innocent seller that's always getting taken, but you see it anyway you wish as long as the C notes keep flowing."

"You oughtn't talk that way out loud," Bug said, "the shoo flies will pounce."

"The only way they pounce is if one of you talk and if you do you'll wind up in the slammer next to me," Sully said. "As far as the Cready wreck, I'll give you this: it's loopy. I read the report after you called and said you were stopping by. I really don't know any more about it than that, but if you pass another C note I can pontificate about what I think."

"Don't stretch your mind too much," Bug said. "There are others in the department that might know more and tell for less."

"Don't think so," Sully said. "I think it's a seller's market this time."

I nodded and slipped a C note out of my pocket and passed it under the desk. If anyone else noticed they didn't say anything and I doubted that they would even if they did notice. My dealings with the cops had taught me that they will put up with info selling as it rarely has a downside to their own efforts. No papers were gonna roll saying a cop had taken a hundred from a private cop, since the two could just say it was a loan, or a payback of a debt or even a friendly wager. Let them catch you taking big money or drug money however and they will fry you thirty ways from Sunday. The cops knew this and acted accordingly, and I was glad they did, cause it wasn't my money but the company's and it saved us a lot of time and shoe leather on some cases.

"What wasn't said in the report," Sully began, smiling since he had made four hundred today, "was that Cready couldn't have picked a worse time to have a wreck. We had a major bus accident out at the intersection of Fourth and Vine. We had to roll all of our forensics people, our medical examiners and most of our street cops. What with the traffic snarl and the fact that there were several deaths, we didn't have time for small accidents, even an accident with a fatality.

"When the guys that did roll got to the Cready accident, it was several hours after the request came in. Further, the forensic guys didn't get out there until the next day, and of course the cops had to release the scene prior to that, so there's a chance the scene would be contaminated."

"The policemen at the scene sent the body of one Mr Randolph Butree back to the morgue and called in to leave a message that the tech that checked on Mr Butree should verify that his body temp made sense. Mr Cready swore that the body was cold when he felt him after the accident. That being said, the body was not checked until the following day as it was a madhouse from all the work going on. There was nothing that said one Mr Butree had not been killed in a car accident, with a broken neck from whiplash and various and other sundry injuries and that's how the tech wrote it up."

Sully stretched, took a sip of coffee and resumed his tale. "The cops at the scene did not see any fresh tyre tracks on the Fuzzy Hill Road, which they felt they should see if Mr Butree was going too fast and was trying to stop before hitting the intersection. They also did not see any fresh tyre tracks that indicated Mr Cready had braked prior to hitting one Butree. They thought that Cready had been going too fast, was likely distracted and ran into Butree as he was pulling out of the intersection."

"Cready said he T-boned the car," Bug interjected. "Ain't that unusual given that Fuzzy Hill is at a dead end into Lancaster. You would expect that the hit car would have been at some angle as he made the turn."

Sully shrugged his shoulders. "I worked a bunch of accidents in my patrol days, you see all sorts of things, and the fact you don't think it should have played out like it did, doesn't mean it didn't play out like it did. Besides, it looked like a common enough accident from the diagram, the Butree car was just beginning to turn when rammed midsection by Cready. Another second or even a half second and Butree would have likely just gotten a nasty headache but as it was he got killed."

"So you gave no credence to Cready's statement that the guy was cold, and to be cold would have had to been dead before the accident?" I asked.

"Not really. Again, why would anyone want to stage an accident for a dead man? What likely happened is that Cready was cagey enough to know that if he could muddy the waters, then the worst that might happen would be that the DA wouldn't want to pursue any charges against him. Now I ain't saying that's the truth of the matter, but I am saying that unless someone comes up with a reason why someone wanted to kill a dead man again in a faked accident, it makes more sense to think Cready is lying or mistaken."

"Yeah," Bug said for no apparent reason, but I understood him. It seemed Cready might be playing us, but even if he was, the law firm was paying us to do this job and we were going to do it.

"As I understand it," I said, "Cready also said he was going over to another accident to try to drum up business for the law firm he had contracts with, but there wasn't any record of an accident out on Higgins Lane. Doesn't it strike you as odd that Cready would give you not one whopper but two? After all, he could have easily said that he was just tooling around looking for accidents. That makes more sense than something that is easily checked and proven false."

"Who knows why anyone does anything?" Sully asked with the eyes of a man that was growing tired of talking and thought he had earned his hundred and I should go about my business.

But I wanted to know his thoughts, and I pressed him. "Well, it is in the report," I said.

"Yes it is," Sully agreed. "But he was likely just making crap up not thinking we would check on him. Cready is a chaser and a chaser never tells the truth when he can think of a lie. I think it's in their union oath or something. Maybe he was up in that area doing some sort of recon on some of the wealthier people in the area or maybe he was looking for a hooker, though that wouldn't be the part of town I'd try, but at any rate, he said what he said and it made no sense. Besides, it may be true. More than one cop has messed with Cready by sending him on a wild goose chase with a fake call. They often enjoy telling of it when they are a few beers over the limit."

"Maybe," I replied. Bug had closed his eyes and appeared to be dozing, which he wasn't but it was a signal to shut up and get out while we were still in somewhat good graces with Sully.

"Well," I said, "regardless of how it turns out, I thank you for your willingness to listen and to help as you can."

"And I appreciate the C note. Keep me in mind at Christmas," Sully said with a grin.

I grinned back, with all the sincerity of a used car salesman.

THE HIDDEN IDENTITIES

The skip trace team wasn't overjoyed to see Starkey. It was bad enough that he had a half dozen phone numbers he wanted run, but he also wanted four identities run too. The three fake IDs he had found at Garson's place and Garson himself. Johnson was the senior data profiler and he glared and growled but eventually said, "We'll try to have you something on the names later today. The phone numbers will be harder, sense we may need a court order for them."

"I'll call them first," Starkey said. "Maybe that'll help some. They're likely burners anyway."

"Yeah and if they're past the limit of when they were first purchased and the first buyer didn't buy more minutes for the phone, then even if you get in touch with someone when you call, it doesn't mean that person had anything to do with the burner phone," Johnson said.

"Damn," Starkey replied. "I didn't know they reused burner phone numbers."

"Only so many numbers to go around," Johnson said. "Now go on and do whatever you want with the phones, as we have real work here that one of our ace detectives has dumped on us."

Starkey went back to his desk and began to call the numbers on the phone. Sure enough he had no luck with the first five, they just rang once and went to no voicemail, which meant they were off, but still active. The sixth was a success, however, and he found himself talking to the head bartender at Smittee's, a joint over on fifth that he had visited a couple of times. As quick as he heard the voice say, "Smittee's" Starkey said, "Oh sorry, dialled the wrong number," and hung up. Then he got out the folder that Transhipments had sent over and picked out a pocket picture of Chuck Garson.

Roach and Bug were just entering the office as Starkey was leaving and Starkey said, "Gotta get a drink and it's on the company's dime and time. Life don't get any better than that."

Bug smiled and said, "Need a partner?"

"On your best day you couldn't be my sidekick," Starkey replied with a smile and before Bug could insult him back he was out the door and on his way to Smittee's.

Starkey drove slowly thinking of baseball and bimbos and not anything about the case, which is how most people spend company time; that is thinking about just about anything but work itself.

Smittee's was a typical bar in a typical city. There was nothing remarkable or unremarkable about it. It was a place where guys went to get drunk and watch sports and the booze wasn't overly expensive but it wasn't all that cheap either. There were two back rooms that could be reserved for "parties". The parties were typically poker games, but the cops didn't ever bust them, even though they were an open secret, because no one gave a damn about drunks losing their money as long as no one got shot in the process.

Starkey entered the bar and headed directly towards the bartender. He had been to the establishment a few times, as he had been in far too many establishments like it a few times. Mostly he just started his night's drinking with a shot or two at a place like this, and then he would go home and really tie one on. Starkey was divorced for some reason.

He sidled up to the bar, said, "Johnny Walker black, neat," and smiled as the bartender replied the same reply Starkey had heard a thousand times, "It certainly is neat." The bartender reached under the bar and pulled out the bottle and filled the shot glass near the rim.

"This stuff is about as close to heaven as a man can get," the bartender said as he placed the glass down before Starkey. "Five bucks please, nobody thinks you can get into heaven for free."

Starkey smiled; a talkative bartender was just what he needed. Starkey pulled out his wallet and took out a fifty and said, "It's all yours and an additional fifty for some information."

"Private copper," the bartender said. "Spotted it right off."

Starkey doubted that but instead pulled another fifty from his wallet, added a five to it for the scotch and then said, "C note for info."

"Maybe," the bartender replied. "I'll take the five and let's hear the pitch for what you want for the hundred. Sometimes an easy hundred is the hardest money you will ever earn, if the person you snitched on finds out you were the snitcher."

"The guy I want info on," Starkey said, "looks more like a choir boy than a mean boy, but you never know, and it's up to you if you want to take the chance."

The bartender shrugged. "Who wants to live forever? Let's hear your pitch."

"I'm looking for this person." Starkey pulled out the picture of Chuck Garson. "I've been told that he used to come in here and that I might be able to get a line on him. As far as I know this is strictly a missing person case, but that's just as far as I know, so take your chances if you talk."

The bartender glanced at the photo and said right away, "No chances to take with that one. He's been in several times but typically sits alone and drowns his sorrows. I think he played poker in the back with some of the boys now and again. Thought his name was Lenny but that could just be a nickname. He always paid in cash. Never ran a tab and never gave me a credit card. He hung around some with Bart Himley and probably others but I know for sure Bart as he comes in here most days around four for a shot or two before going home to the missus. You're welcome to wait for him, particularly if you continue to buy Johnny Walker. I will now pocket the hundred bucks."

"Well, since I can't put more than one drink on my expense voucher, make it the cheap stuff instead," Starkey said. "I'll be over at the back table next to the bathrooms. When Mr Himley comes in give me the high sign."

"Another fifty?" the bartender asked.

"Sure," Starkey replied and pulled his wallet out and handed over another fifty. Starkey walked to the back of the bar, sat down and deliberately sipped the booze the bartender brought, because he didn't want to get drunk and that was always a temptation when one was stupid enough to hang out in a bar.

Time passed slowly because it was a mid-afternoon weekday, therefore the two TVs were tuned to different news programs and not sports. Starkey didn't know why, but for some reason booze tasted better when you were watching baseball or football, which was why sports bars existed. Or maybe people just thought the booze tasted better and the sports was just another excuse for tying one on.

Time passed more slowly. Starkey pulled out a book he always carried just for situations like this. An investigator spends about as much time waiting for things to happen as he does doing things when they do happen. Maybe most jobs were like that, where the prep was longer than the doing. Regardless, one became a reader since that was cheap and passed the time and wasn't dependent upon wifi.

The clock finally hit the magic 4 p.m. and no more than one minute later a fat guy, wearing a hat with a feather in the band entered the bar. The bartender said loudly, "Hi Bart," and nodded towards Starkey. "A private peeper wants to talk to you about Lenny."

That wasn't exactly the high sign Starkey had in mind, since he wasn't sure he wanted his information source to know he was copper, private or not, but Starkey just nodded at the bartender and Mr Himley and indicated with his hand that he wanted Himley to sit at his table. Himley nodded back, walked over and asked, "If you're buying, I'm sitting."

"Then by all means sit," Starkey said and motioned for the bartender to bring some drinks over. "Thanks for your time. This shouldn't take but a few minutes."

"As long as you're buying it can take all night," Himley said. "By the way, who exactly are you and what exactly do you expect for the booze I am about to consume?"

"I'm an investigator for the National Detective Agency," Starkey replied and pulled his identification from his pocket. "I'm looking for this individual, Mr Chuck Garson." He put the photo of Chuck Garson on the table and watched closely to see if it brought any reaction from Himley.

"Lenny," Himley said. "We all called him Lenny, thought it was his name but I guess it wasn't. Never heard his last name."

Starkey had noted that one of the fake IDs had the name Leonard Rydell on it. Now that he knew which fake ID was being used here, Starkey needed to figure out why.

"How well did you know Lenny?" Starkey asked.

"No more than the next guy in a bar," Himley replied and finished his drink. "Talking is thirsty work."

Starkey wanted to say, you ain't done all that much talking yet, but held his peace and shouted out to the bartender, "Bring over a bottle. Me and Bart are about to become best buds." Starkey smiled broadly as he spoke.

"I like the way you do your interview work," Himley replied. "Not that I've had any experience at being interviewed, since all I do for a living is run a locksmith shop. But this type of interviewing can go on for as long as I'm sober."

The bartender arrived with a bottle and said, "Fifty bucks or a credit card. Plus a tip for the effort." But he said it with a big smile like it was a joke, even though it wasn't.

Starkey had a company credit card and pulled it out and handed it to the bartender. "Give yourself twenty for the tip. National can afford it."

"Good doing business with you," the bartender said as he took the credit card away. "And I ain't just whistling when I say that, brother."

Himley didn't waste any time hitting the bottle and had poured himself a stiff one before the bartender had even left. "Thanks, and as the bartender said, I ain't just whistling, brother."

"No problem," Starkey replied. "It's a little known fact but it's the truth. A man ain't nearly as stingy when he's spending his boss's money. Now exactly what did you know about Lenny? For instance, did you know what he did for a living?"

"Nah," Himley said as he poured himself another drink. The boss wasn't gonna like Starkey's expense report. "Didn't know hardly anything about him, except he came in here often. We played some pool once in a while and played a lot of poker. He had some sort of job I'm sure, cause he would say he had to get home cause he had to work the next day, but usually that was when he was up in poker and that's a dodge that's likely as old as poker itself."

"What did he talk about with you?" Starkey asked.

"Usual stuff, girls, sports, some politics but not much," Himley replied. "You know bar talk. It starts off as mutual insults then goes downhill from there. Just guy talk. Not really anything about the guy's life of course, unless he has decided to make up a fairy tale or two."

"Ever go anywhere else with him?" Starkey asked.

"No. It ain't like we met here, we just happened to be here at the same time, and we were killing time. And it wasn't just him and me, we both would just hang around with any other regulars that happen to be about."

"Do you know where he lived?" Starkey asked.

"No," Himley replied and hit the bottle again.

"And you never heard anyone call him Chuck or Garson?"

"Again no. I just knew him as Lenny. The bartender, Sacks over there, might have known his last name, but I doubt it. From what I can recall Lenny was strictly a cash fellow and didn't run a tab or use a credit card."

"You never had any dealings with him outside of this place? Or do you know if any others that had dealings with him outside of the bar?"

"No and no," Himley replied. His words were beginning to slur a bit and Starkey was pretty sure he'd gotten as much out of Himley as he was going to, at least for the present.

"Tell you what," Himley continued, "the poker game starts up back in room 2 over there," he pointed towards the left room by the bathroom. "At about 9 p.m., it generally runs to midnight as long as there are players and there usually are. Come on back tonight and I will introduce you to some of the other guys that knew Lenny. I ain't sure you'll get anything out of 'em, but if you're willing to buy their booze they'll at least hear you out."

"Thanks," Starkey said. "I'll come back at nine, with my credit card." He got up from the table and noticed the bottle was still half full, which meant it was half empty and he hadn't had a drop. "You okay to get home?" he asked Himley.

"I ain't going home," Himley responded and smiled lopsided. "Unless you are taking this here bottle with your own true self."

"Keep it," Starkey said, "And thanks for trying to help." He picked up his credit card from Sacks the bartender and said, "Himley seems to be fairly lit. Might want to make sure he doesn't drive."

"Himley is often lit," Sacks said. "And he doesn't drive that I know of; he walks home and it ain't but a couple of blocks away. Thanks for being concerned however."

Starkey nodded and headed out of the bar. He'd be back at 9 p.m. and the only thing he was convinced of was that Himley and Sacks were both lying about their relationship with Leonard or Chuck or whatever ID Garson had chosen to use when he was in this place.

SKIP TRACE IS OUR FRIEND

I was tasting a cup of really bad coffee when the intern brought up the skip trace report we'd asked for on Butree. The intern was a young man majoring in criminal justice at the local university and he would likely be a hell of a man catcher one day, if he went with the FBI or something. If he stayed here he would wind up fat, broke and pushing fifty like the rest of us. His initials were J.D. That's what everybody called him.

"Your report on one Mr Butree," the lad said. "Is there anything else the skip trace team can do for the mighty detective Roach?"

"You gotta work here for more than three months before you call me Roach," I said. "It's either Mr Roche or his highness the king of detectives, whichever you prefer. Now go and chase your electrons on the computer like a good little boy, and pray that you to may one day become a mighty detective like your betters."

"Don't think that's all that great an accomplishment," J.D. said. "Considering the quality of the people around here."

I opened the report and began to read. I really didn't have time for more insults, besides the kid was better at it than me, so I just said, "Run back to skip trace, I'm sure your computer is going through withdrawal without the gentle caress of your fingers."

That drew a loud guffaw from the retreating figure, but no reply so it looked like I had one of my rare victories in the repartee battles that were a daily part of our work life.

The skip trace report was a doozy and I do mean it couldn't be more doozier. This Mr Randolph Butree had been a busy fellow during his shortish life, having passed away at the ripe old age of thirty-five. The man had a technical degree in electronics from some college I had not heard of, which wasn't surprising, but the fact he had served five years for burglary was.

His rap sheet showed several arrests, many more interrogations, two trials and one conviction. The dossier further described that Butree was suspected of several unsolved bank robberies over the past few years, ever since he had gotten out of stir. Evidently he'd found that the profits from bank robbery were higher than for burglary, he had also likely found that pulling a job once a year exposed you to less of a chance to go back in the slammer than did pulling a job once a month which was typical of burglars.

Butree was an expert on intrusion detection systems and had actually once worked as an installer of the very same systems he was now disabling. The report said he was not tied up with any specific mob but was a floater and would work with any group that he felt comfortable with. He was not married and did not live extravagantly, but the feds thought he had a hideaway somewhere that he intended to retreat to once he had enough money to retire from the rackets. It was rumoured he had a Swiss bank account, but only rumoured, since the Swiss wouldn't give up any information to save the world from a holocaust much less because the FBI wanted the info.

I noted Butree's local address; a small apartment in a complex I had visited more than once. It wasn't high rent, but it wasn't a hovel either. Me and Bug would slip over there after dark and see if we could bribe the super to let us in and if that failed, we might get Sully interested enough to have the cops look it over. If both options failed, then I'd get Bug to sneak in while I was on lookout, but I really didn't want to go that far unless I had to.

Bug was just walking back to his desk from either a meeting or a bathroom break as he had that look of having completed some unpleasant task, you know, the "thank God that's through look".

"Bug, my lad, our life just got interesting," I said and tossed the report at him. "Read that and tell me how you like them apples."

"Ugh," was Bug's reply, which was often his reply to any news I found exciting, cause Bug, regardless of his other qualities, was not an excitement kind of person.

I drank some more bad coffee while Bug digested the skip trace report. I thought I saw him smile, but knowing Bug it was more likely indigestion. Finally he put the report down and said, "That does make one think. What's the odds that a thief would be involved in a car wreck that seems to be hinkey? Smallish to none. Of course, Cready might have known that Butree was of the criminal class and made up the hinkey stuff afterward. Which way do you bet?"

"Until our client, or at least our subject," I said, "since the law firm is really our client, until Cready proves to have lied, or manufactured evidence, then I go with him. What say we high tail it over to Butree's place and see if we can buy our way in?"

"Sounds like a plan. By the way, First National was hit on the fifteenth, I think I saw on one of our daily briefs."

"Yeah," I replied, "I remembered that. I had a wild thought that I need to get skip trace on. Meet you at the car."

Bug grunted and pushed back from his chair with a grunt that showed his age and a grimace that showed his ageing bones. I know because I made the same grunt and grimace for the same reason.

I went down to skip trace, saw J.D. was looking at something that looked a lot like YouTube and said, "You ain't gonna get ahead that way, J.D."

"I ain't gonna get ahead anyway," he said. "Besides, it's my break."

"Well, when you get off break I need to know the location of all accidents on the fifteenth in our fair city," I said. "If you can't find it, let me know and I'll hit up the cops, but I'd rather they not know what I'm doing yet."

"Don't worry," J.D. replied. "I'll find it."

I left the enterprising young lad hunched over his computer and typing furiously and headed to the garage. Bug had already checked out a car and was waiting for me as I got there.

He drove silently and I let him be silent as I was thinking about the case and seeing if the parts fit. Thus far the parts seemed to be falling in place but proving they fit would be a whole other kettle of fish.

As we pulled up to the apartment complex, I knew we were too late and I knew we weren't going in. I saw a couple of detectives I knew on stake-out. Now that might be a coincidence and then again Odin might just be the god of all gods, but I thought the latter was more likely to be true than the former.

"Couple of detectives," I said to Bug. "Over in that Ford SUV, Styles and Ramirez, if memory serves. Just keep on travelling, Bug."

"Ugh," Bug said which was his favourite word, and an all-purpose word that meant whatever it was Bug wanted it to mean.

After we had gotten a good fifteen minutes away from the apartment I said, "Let's grab a beer and discuss the wherefores, Bug."

"Ugh," he said once more and pulled into the next bar that he saw. Within moments we had a cold one before us and I began to palaver.

"Here's how I see it so far," I said. "Jump in if you think something is amiss." I took a moment to take a sip of the beer, and didn't really like the taste but what the hell, everyone thought I was a drinker because you are supposed to be a drinker if you're a cop, so I kept on drinking.

"I read it this way and even if it sounds dopey," I began, "it's still the way it reads. One Randolph Butree was involved in the First National heist on the fifteenth. After the heist he dies, probably in a car accident since that's what his partners went to a lot of trouble to recreate." I looked at Bug to make sure he was following and if he saw any holes, then continued, "They set up Cready, probably no malice there, it's just they knew he was a chaser and would likely be out where they could put him in the right place at the right time.

"They probably got a cop or two on the take. Makes sense that they asked the cop to call Cready and send him into their little trap. They spring the trap, it works. Cready takes the rap for the death of Butree. Any objections so far, outside of why, which we ain't got a clue?"

"Was there a question somewhere in that sentence?" Bug asked.

I smiled. "I don't know why they did it, but I have hopes of finding out."

"You know," Bug replied, his face in deep thought, "there's a $100,000 reward for info leading to the recovery of the loot. Half of that would be a nice addition to my 401K."

"Like you got a 401K" I replied. "But I agree that $50,000 will soothe me on long lonely nights, assuming National lets us keep it. You know the rules, if we stumble on something then we get to keep the reward, if we turn it up as part of our investigation, then it belongs to National. Since our primary concern is helping Cready, then we may be alright. But let's keep the connection between the robbery and the accident—if there is a connection—to ourselves for a little while."

"Wonder why Sully didn't mention that Butree was a crook?" Bug asked.

"One, he might not have known. Two, he might have known and didn't think it was significant; three, he might have known and withheld the information thinking he could sell it to us or someone else later."

"Okay," Bug said. "And the cops think Butree was part of the mob that robbed First National. They have his place staked out, looking for him or any of his known associates. If they knew he was dead, then they wouldn't be there. Ipso facto, the detectives don't know about the accident ..."

"Exactly," I agreed. "They will likely find out sooner rather than later, but it's for sure they don't know a thing now. It's also sure that they have searched Butree's apartment and found anything that we might need, so we can get it from them if need be, and it is also sure, they'll haul us in if we try to go anywhere near Butree's apartment, so that's out."

"Say that Butree was dead," Bug said. "They had to keep the body refrigerated to prevent decay, as some decay sets in almost immediately. We might see if we can find a connection with some place that has a big enough freezer to hold a man as large as Butree."

"Yes indeedy," I replied. "And we can also look for another car accident, likely a hit and run, that happened the night before Cready's accident and after the bank job. From what I recall, that would make it around 5 or 6 in the morning of the fifteenth. I already got skip trace checking on it for us."

"That calls for a drink," Bug said and he held up his beer. "To fifty grand, and a hell of a trip to Vegas when our ship comes in."

POKER OR SOMETHING LIKE THAT

Starkey was back at Smittee's by 8.30 p.m. and had already grabbed a bottle for himself and was nursing same when he saw Himley arrive. Himley waved and nodded towards the room he had indicated earlier. As he walked towards the room, Starkey grabbed his bottle, saying, "Come on, baby, time to earn your keep," and hurried to catch up with Himley.

They entered the room with Himley leading, and immediately there was quiet, more quiet than Starkey thought was usual. Maybe the room had some soundproofing, just for that reason, Starkey thought, but then he usually thought the worse reason for most anything. It came from twenty years of thinking the worse, and being proved an optimist.

"This," Himley said, "is the poker room, though if any cops come around Sacks calls it the meeting room. We pay Sacks a hundred bucks each night to use it. Sometimes we even have meetings here, so I guess Sacks ain't lying when he calls it that."

"And you say that Garson, or Leonard Rydell as you knew him, used to play poker here with you and others," Starkey said.

"Well, kinda poker, sometimes we played gin rummy, sometimes euchre, sometimes rook, always some card game though never dice. It's just penny ante stuff, the average pot was say hundred bucks, the largest I ever saw was $500 and some. The game was never meant to be big stakes, just a way to have some drinks, cuss, smoke cigars, sometimes run porn on that TV in the corner, you know, guys night-out type stuff, but a cheap night out all the same."

"Who generally played with you?" Starkey asked.

"Usually Bigg Jones and Tom Wreek, at a minimum," Himley said. "They'll be here shortly if they follow their usual pattern. Of course, we usually have a fifth and sometimes a sixth player but they would usually just be whoever in the bar wanted to come in and play. I ain't saying we were as regular as rain with our foursome, but most Thursday nights, we'd wind up here. Generally we'd break up around 1 or 2 a.m., but I recall a time or two we went all night."

Just as Himley was finishing his description of the card game routine the door opened and two men entered. One was a large man, at least six foot four inches, really heavy at close to 300 pounds, and he was evidently carrying a gun under his too-close-fitting jacket. The other was a much smaller man, maybe five foot ten inches and perhaps 180. The big man looked to be about forty; the young man no more than thirty. They both nodded at Himley and looked at Starkey with cold and questioning eyes.

"As I was just saying," Himley continued, "Bigg and Tom here are some of our regulars. Bigg is the big un, I expect his real name ain't Bigg but everybody I know calls him that and whatever his real moniker is he keeps to hisself, and Tom is the regular size fellow. Guys, meet Mr Starkey here, he's a private cop looking for Lenny."

There was no surprise in their eyes when Himley told them he was a private cop, so Starkey was pretty sure they expected him, even though they tried to act surprised. Starkey stuck his hand out and shook first Tom's and then Bigg's and was surprised that Bigg's hand was not larger than it was.

Bigg said, "What'cha want to know about Lenny and if I tell you anything will it get me or Lenny in trouble, and particularly me?"

Starkey pulled the picture of Garson from his pocket and said, "I don't expect it will get either of you in trouble, unless you know something I don't know. This man you call Lenny, is this the picture of him?"

Both Bigg and Tom nodded.

"His real name, or at least what I think is his real name, is Chuck Garson, and he works for a firm that has hired me to find him. Chuck/Lenny has not shown up for work in the past three days and his company is worried for his safety." The company could care less about his safety if they found the Swiss bank numbers that Garson had been skimming, but Starkey kept that fact to himself.

Tom said, "I don't know anything about Lenny, except that he plays bad poker and worse gin rummy, which means we liked for him to sit in at cards. Outside of that, I couldn't tell you a thing."

Bigg nodded. "That's about all. Lenny was quick with a joke, quicker to pass on a full house, and as far as I could tell could hold his liquor as well as the next guy, but I knew nothing about any other part of his life."

Starkey nodded at both of them. "Here's my card." He handed one of his cards to each of them. "If you think of something, give me a call. I can't guarantee you any money but the company is talking about offering a reward."

They both smiled and nodded. Starkey figured the cards would go right into the trash as he walked out, then he put the rest of his scotch bottle on the table and said, "For services thus rendered." Then he shook hands all around and left.

As he drove, Starkey kept watch for a tail but didn't see one; that didn't mean there wasn't a tail, but if there was one, the tailer was more expert in the tailing than Starkey was at seeing the tail. He wasn't sure what went on in the poker room, but he didn't think it was a whole lotta poker. The poker chips for instance were all nice and new. The floor was clean. While he had smelled some cigar smoke, he didn't think it was smoke that had accumulated over four or five years and multiple nights.

Starkey took an extra half dozen turns and ran a few stop signs before he convinced himself he was safe to go home. At the last minute, he decided on one more double back, and was glad he had, as he saw the man that had been identified to him as Tom Wreek driving the other way, trying his best not to be noticed.

That was some professional tail, and Starkey did not want to give his home away. Instead he drove to a hotel that the National Detective Agency used for instances such as this, and got one of the company rooms. Starkey did not know if this Tom Wreek was looking to find Garson or was looking to take a potshot at the fine National Agent known as Starkey. He assumed the former but could not rule out the latter.

Once Starkey had checked in, he immediately called Thompson, who wasn't overly glad to hear from an agent at 10 p.m. but it happened so often Thompson only bitched about it for five minutes.

After five minutes of bitching started to turn into more Starkey cut him off and said, "I know, it's late, your wife doesn't understand you and the world ain't fair, but I still gotta get these guys checked out. They either know where Garson is and want to take me out of the picture so I don't find him, or else they want me to lead them to Garson. Either way, I don't want them to know where I am."

"Well," Thompson said, "I'll sign off on the charges and assign them to Transhipment, so it's okay you went to ground. You need some backup?"

"Not yet," Starkey replied. "Have skip trace run these three names. I'll likely not come in to the office for the next day or two, as I don't want them to find me until I know more about what they are up to so have them call me and debrief me."

"Okay," Thompson said. "Get some sleep and we'll check on your place a few times to see if they break in. If they do we'll get the cops on them and that might loosen their tongues."

"I don't think so," Starkey replied. "I wasn't all that sure that Himley was a crook, as he didn't talk or act like one, but the guy called Bigg I know from a previous bust. He's a muscle guy for hire, as I understand it—if you want someone slammed on the chin, he will be glad to do the slamming for a few C notes, of course. The one called Tom Wreek, I don't know, but he was so slick at tailing me that I bet he's a driver."

"Okay," Thompson said. "I'll get skip trace on it first thing tomorrow. You might want to go by and see Sully and try to pump him on this Garson case. He might know of a connection, though I have to admit I don't see one on the surface."

"Nor do I, but there's something there. I think it likely that they're looking for Garson, since otherwise I don't think Sacks and Himley would have ever acknowledged they knew him. But it's just my hunch, cause you never know how someone is playing you until the play is over, and sometimes not even then."

"As I said," Thompson said, "get some sleep. We'll get the info to you as quickly as possible. Fill me in on anything else you gather over the next day or two, and I'll cover for you at the office."

"Thanks," Starkey replied and hung up.

The company hotel room had all of the amenities, including toothbrush, an electric shaver, and even pyjamas. It was meant for customers, of course, someone who needed to hide out from a warrant that was going to be served, or to hide from the cops until the story was set on what to tell the cops. It had a lot of things, but it held no sleep for Starkey that night.

He tossed and turned, taking a moment to turn the TV on then off, then tossed some more and turned some more. He hated these kind of cases, where he was matching wits with the crooks. Starkey was too old and had done way too many cases to look for the challenging ones. The unchallenging ones paid the same and were easier on the nerves.

Sometime in the morning, he finally closed his eyes and it struck. Just as sleep was taking over his mind it struck him, like a bolt from the blue—Garson was an expert of Swiss banking. And just that quickly the sleep ran away from him.

If he could find what criminal activity that Mr Himley, Mr Jones and Mr Wreek had committed or intended to commit, then he would likely find the connection with Garson. It wouldn't be the first time that crooks had laundered their money through a Swiss bank, and it wouldn't be the first time that the guy doing the laundering took off with the loot.

With a smile on his lips, Starkey heaved a sigh, got out of bed and wrote his report, making sure he described what he thought the connection was. As quick as he finished the report he was as sleepy as hell, but the breaking dawn meant he was out of luck this night.

MU—THE MYSTERY GETS MUDDLED

There are three types of people. Those that see the glass of whiskey half full. Those that see the glass of whiskey half empty. Those that drink the glass, regardless of half full or half empty, then look for the bottle and drink that also. I like to think that's the kinda guy I am.

—The wisdom (or lack thereof) of Bug

NOT ALL ACCIDENTS ARE CREATED EQUAL

Bug and I got back to the office about 2 p.m., one of those crappy times where it's too early to go home and too late to do a whole lot of investigating. We went to our separate desks and waited on the report I had requested. Sure enough, we had no more than sat down when J.D. came hustling over. "Not all accidents are equal, you know," he said, "so as an A1 detective, I've identified two of the fourteen on the list that you should look into first."

J.D. was young and still cared and I didn't want to prick his balloon but I would do my own sorting and assembling, thanks anyway. I let him go on showing his college smarts.

"There were a total of fourteen accidents reported on the fifteenth between 1 a.m. and 6 a.m. in this fair city of ours. While that sounds like a lot, you will recall that there was a huge rain storm at the time, and that ups the probability of accidents by about fourfold. Of those fourteen accidents, twelve were reported by 4 a.m., so they happened prior to 4 a.m., how's that for logic?"

"A real detective couldn't do it any better," I admitted.

J.D. smiled that boyish smile that probably sent the lasses into delirium but was just grating to an old guy like me. "The other two were reported after 5 a.m., after day break really," he continued, "but the accidents themselves were said to have happened between 5 and 6 a.m., so those two fit more precisely the criteria you gave me."

"Why did you report the other twelve then?" Bug asked.

"Cause you guys would holler at me if I didn't choose something that could have been what you wanted. And Roach's words were, I am most interested in accidents between 5 and 6 a.m. but will take anything after 1 a.m. Ain't that right, Roach?"

"That's Roche to you, kid," I said. "But yeah I told him those precise words. We just got a feeling right now, Bug, and it may be that the accident we need to investigate doesn't tie in at all with the other thing we discussed." I didn't say robbery out loud because J.D. had big ears and a bigger mouth, and he would skedaddle to Thompson if he thought he could earn a brownie point or two.

"See," the kid said and I swear I thought he was gonna stick his tongue out at Bug but he didn't. "Here are all fourteen accidents that were reported to the police. You great detectives go and do your magic with them."

"Thanks, J.D.," I said and even though I meant it I couldn't let him escape without an insult or he might have thought something was up, "Now go on back to your romper room and play with your toys."

I scanned the accident reports and it was easy to do. Each listing was only a few sentences, stating the names of those involved and whether there were any casualties. While J. D. was right in his assumption that the only two I was really concerned with were the two between 5 and 6 a.m., if he had known more, he could have narrowed it to one. Only one of the two we looked at was involved both a fatality and a hit and run. If my hunch was right, that was the mother lode.

"Come on, Bug," I said. "We might get some overtime today. I want to check out the location where this final accident took place. It's over at Fourth and Garvin. We may be able to see if we can find some stray camera that will provide us all the info we need."

"Can't it wait till tomorrow?" Bug said. "I gotta date tonight."

"Yeah," I replied, "with Agnes no doubt." This was likely as Agnes was his cat and I swore he loved that feline more than a man loves his bride on his wedding night.

"No," Bug said, "this is with a real woman, and she ain't bought and paid for like one of Starkey's. Have a heart."

Knowing Bug, that was probably hooey, but what the hell, it didn't take two people to look over one site. "Okay, you just talked your way out of one exciting trip. If it is a real girl and not a rubber doll, say hi for me and see if she's got a friend."

"If she had a friend," Bug said, "she wouldn't keep her as one if she introduced her to you."

There was truth to that so I just smiled and walked off to requisition a car. It was my luck that all of the decent ones had been checked out and I was stuck with a small compact that I could barely fit into. I started to take my own car instead, but changed my mind—I didn't want any cop to spot me and more importantly my tag number that could lead him to me. Small chance, but then $50,000 was at stake.

Fourth and Garvin was in the southwest side of the city. I noted it was only four blocks from the First National bank that had been hit on the fifteenth. That was another good reason to check on the site.

The accident had been cleared away, so the trip to the site was strictly to see if I could figure out who hit who and where trash wound up. I had found, more than once, debris from an accident that had just been swept to the side and ignored by the cops.

There were several cameras around the intersection and I thought the one at the nightclub looked promising. The club was called the Night of Colours and the parking lot camera I spotted was facing the intersection where the wreck had happened. I didn't doubt that the cops had already got a copy, after all there had been a death in the hit and run here, but the club might be willing to give me a copy for fifty or even free, and that would beat paying Sully a hundred for it.

I parked in the lot of the Night of Colours easily enough. It was an all-day parking lot, which charged $25 regardless of how long you stayed there. The sign stated that the lot had to be empty by 7 p.m. or you risked having your car towed, that was when the Night of Colours started their nightly drunk traffic I suspected.

I walked over to the corner of Fourth and Garvin, the north corner to be precise. Any indication of a wreck had long since disappeared from the streets. The cops would have released the site as quickly as feasible, since this was a busy downtown intersection, but I had hopes for one of the two alleys that were fairly close to the intersection.

The first alley I tried yielded nothing but empty garbage cans. Evidently the trash guys had collected not too much earlier than my arrival. I saw an old wino at the end of the alley, already blotto at 3 p.m. I started to go down and ask him a question or two, just to give him a twenty spot, but he was drunk and I didn't want to ruin his buzz. Besides, if he smelled half as bad as he looked I didn't want to ruin my nostrils.

I crossed the street at the next red light and made sure to cross only on the walk sign. The cops weren't likely to have this place under surveillance, but no need taking any chances as I had plenty of time, what with our services guaranteed for at least two weeks. There was another alley there, and it didn't look much different from the one I just left, except there didn't seem to be a wino holed up at the far end. I walked several feet into the alley and saw a lot of debris from possibly various wrecks, but I picked up what looked like a busted tail light. I'd get Jonathan to see if he could identify the car it came from if I couldn't get any camera footage.

Outside of that piece of debris and the wino, whose sight had made me glad again that I was just a fake drinker at best, the physical scene had not yielded any great clues, but then I hadn't expected it to. But seeing the sight, I solidified my thoughts and if what I expected happened then, the guys from the robbery had been proceeding north and the car they had collided with, which was owned by one Jeremy Travers, was coming east. One of them ran the stop light, probably the crooks, but I wouldn't know unless I found the footage.

The wreck had been severe enough to kill Travers, and likely it killed Butree. Since the crooks weren't likely to stick around with a trunk full of stolen loot, they had beat it, adding hit and run to their other crimes against humanity.

I walked back across the street, again with the light, dropped the tail light piece into the trunk of my car, then walked over to see the parking lot attendant. He was a young guy who looked bored. He was having a fine old time on his phone, probably beating the fifteenth level of some obscure video game. His face was more intent on capturing the next game piece than most men I had seen when they captured some miscreant on the top ten wanted list.

"Hello," I said and pulled my wallet out. "Care to make twenty bucks?"

He put his phone down and gave me a look of disdain, as if to say, go away, codger, you bother me. "What can I do for you, sir?" he asked in a voice that was flat and without interest.

"There was a wreck at that intersection," I said. "About a week ago, on the fifteenth. It happened about 5 in the morning, or at least that's what the accident report said. I thought you might have caught the clean-up, if you happened to be working that day."

"I caught it," he said. "And I'll take your twenty. Private cop, huh?"

"Yes," I said as I passed the twenty over to him.

"Had to be. The cops don't pass out any money when they want some info, they just threaten you with the pokey if you clam up."

He smiled as he took the twenty, which was likely equal to three or four hours of take home pay to him, which made me glad I wasn't a kid anymore and could earn some sort of a living, even if it was at the expense of grunting every time you got out of a chair.

"Not a whole lot to tell," the kid said. "I missed the wreck itself, as probably most people that work for a living did. This place really doesn't start to wake up till seven, and I don't get to work until 7.15 a.m., at least most days. But I did see some of the clean-up." He pointed to the intersection. "There was a beamer that looked like it had been crushed by a much bigger car. Some poor guy bought it in the crash. Whoever was in the other car must have been injured too, as I heard the cops talk about blood being over away from the beamer and it wasn't likely the blood of the deceased.

"They came over and talked to me," the kid continued, "when they saw me unlock the gate to the parking lot. They figured I'd know if there were any folks that would have been around during the time the wreck occurred. The only one I could think of was Jimmy, he runs a newsstand right around the corner of fourth, and he might have heard the wreck and come to look at it. You might want to try him as well."

"Right around which corner?" I asked.

The kid pointed towards the east side and I wrote it down.

"I notice the camera you have up there," I said and pointed towards it. "Can I get the footage from that camera for the time that the accident happened?"

"Sorry, pops. You'll have to take that up with Jake Rothlein, at least I think his last name is Rothlein. The camera belongs to the nightclub over there, Night of Colours. Jake runs security for them, and it's their camera. I think they cut it on around 6 p.m. and it runs through the night, but I can't say for sure, it's just what I've heard. Jake's let me in the club a few times when they have a light crowd."

"So, when will Jake be in?" I asked.

"Usually gets in at 4.30 or so," the kid replied. "I usually leave at 6 p.m. so I see him most days, and he always waves. I'm sure if that twenty of yours has brothers, then Jake will be delighted to see you."

I nodded and thought the kid was right, people will talk sometimes out of the goodness of their heart, but to get them to really spill the beans, you need to dangle a bit of an inducement in front of them.

"I'll be back about 4.30," I said. "I think I'll zip over to see the newsstand operator, if he's still around."

"He probably is. I think he sells a lot of snacks up to about 3 p.m., then business slacks off since people are too busy finishing up work, or they don't want to ruin their dinner. Tell him Joey sent you. That'll help."

"Thanks, Joey," I said as I started to walk away.

"My name ain't Joey, it's Marvin, but Jimmy don't like me over much. Joey is the owner and he operates this thing about as much as I do."

"Then thanks, Marvin," I said with a grin. The kid smiled back and immediately grabbed his phone for the next level of Gotta Smakem or whatever it is that youngsters play on their phones these days.

I walked over to the corner and crossed and then around to the area where Marvin had pointed. There was a small stand there, with soft drinks, candy bars, newspapers, magazines, that type of stuff. There was an old grey-haired guy sitting in a straight-backed high chair, looking off into the distance and I figured that was Jimmy. I ambled over to the stand and grabbed a magazine and put it on the counter in front of the old man.

"I'll take this and as much info as twenty bucks will get me," I said. "That's if you're Jimmy."

"Jimmy's what they calls me," he said. "And you can sure buy that magazine, but twenty don't buy no whole lot of info, at least not as much as fifty buys."

I figured Jimmy had been pumped more than once in his career, after all, he was on the corner of a busy street and there were lawyers, chasers and various and sundry private coppers that were often interested in things that happen on that street. Doubtless he had negotiated that price before and expected to get it again, and he got it.

I took two twenties and a ten from my wallet and passed them over along with a ten spot for the magazine, which I didn't want but since I was paying for it I was damn well gonna keep it. Jimmy worked out my change for the magazine and put it in my hand and then pocketed the fifty, not putting it into the cash register.

"You has bought yourself some info, what can I do for you?" he asked, and you got me where that dialect came from.

"There was a wreck up on the intersection of the fifteenth at around 5 a.m., and it was during a rain storm, so I really don't know if you were open, but if you were, did you see or hear anything?"

"Saw a little, heard lots more," Jimmy said. "It was raining worsen you expect but no more than you deserve I suspect, and I was sitting here under my umbrella." He nodded at the umbrella that protected his small stand from rain and from sunlight. "Didn't have anything out yet, cause it was early and it was raining. But I gotch nuttin else to do anyway so I was just setting here waiting for the rain to stop. Suddenly I sees this BMW whip by my stand and it look like the driver ain't feeling no pain if you knows what I mean, but I only caught a glimpse so I may be doing the guy a misdeed by saying that as I ain't sure. But it looked like he was looped."

Jimmy stopped and pointed down towards the intersection. "Next thing I hear a crash, didn't hear no squealing brakes either, just a crash. I think the BMW done ploughed into something, and it sure has."

He returned his gaze to me and continued, "I got out my smaller umbrella and I headed down to see if I could help anybody that was hurt. I got there within a minute of the accident, but the other car was pulling away, even though it was busted up plenty. I tried to get the licence number but I can't see for crap anymore and it was raining so I couldn't see it. It was an SUV, I think a Ford but as God is my witness I don't know one from anotherin. I ran to the BMW and saw that it was all stoved up, and that the guy that I thought had been feeling no pain had just felt a bunch. I looked at him and I thought he was dead right then, but can't swear he was. But it didn't matter as he was wedged tight in that little cuss of a car and I sure warn't gonna be able to pull him out.

"So, I calls the cop," Jimmy continued, "and told them there was a hit and run and one guy's more than likely dead and to come on over and bring an ambulance. That's about it. Wished to God I'd seen more, nothing I hate worse than a hit and run. Likely it was hippies."

I looked at him to make sure I understood his last statement, and I had. Somehow, at least in his world, the label of hippies was the ultimate insult. It likely was in mine too now that I thought about it.

I thanked Jimmy and wandered back to the Night of Colours nightclub. I got there just in time to see

Marvin the lot attendant point me out to the person I took to be Jake, the guy that worked security. If ever a man could run security, my money was on Jake. He was at least 250 and it seemed all muscle in the tight fitting shirt and jeans he was wearing. The only thing that ruined his look of physical perfection was a set of eyeglasses that were stylish, but still seemed out of place on a body such as that.

Jake waved me over and said, "Understand you're a guy that likes to spread the joy. I'm the kind that likes to receive joy, so we should get along great." He extended his hand and I shook it. After that speech, I had to resist the temptation to look at my hand, just to make sure Jake hadn't stolen a finger or two.

"Yeah," I replied, "I'm a private cop, I work for National Detective if that matters overly much to you. I even have a couple of cards on me, which do you want, the one that says I'm Guy Stevens or the one that says I'm Lucas Albree?"

"A private cop that don't want his identity known," Jake said. "No problem as I ain't never met you before and am not likely to remember you after our business is concluded, so keep your cards. Let's you and me go over to my little ole place of business and see how many of those Andrew Jacksons I can wrangle out of you."

I didn't know exactly how to take this Jake, as he seemed much more free and open than most security people I dealt with. Usually people that handle security keep their mouth shut but good until they see if the money they were gonna get was worth the grief they might get for providing the info. On the other hand, Marvin had likely filled him in on what I needed, the footage from the camera on a given night, and there is definitely no way that providing said footage could be illegal, and therefore Jake wasn't likely to get any trouble for the release.

I followed Jake as he unlocked the outer door, then the inner door, snapped on a couple of lights, then walked to an office at the back of the dance floor and then he unlocked that door as well. All I can say is this was one security person that took security seriously.

"You want a free drink?" Jake asked. "The conglomerate that owns this place can afford it, and the manager wouldn't know it was missing even if he saw you drink it."

"Help yourself," I said, "but I'm on duty, and even though I'm not a real taxpayer cop, I'm still a cop and I try to take it seriously."

"I can't either," Jake replied, "cause I hate the stuff. It's ruined the life of many a good man, and bad one too likely, but that aside, it just tastes lousy and it gives me a headache. That's likely why I'm security here, the manager knows at least I ain't gonna drink all the profit up. Have a seat, and let's talk of those Andy Jacksons."

"Word does get around," I replied. "There was a wreck at the intersection on the morning of the fifteenth. Don't know if you saw it as it was around 5 a.m. when it happened, but I thought maybe your camera had caught it. I've been hired to find out who the hit and run driver was. I can make sure you get a C note right now if you give me the footage and can arrange to pay you another C note if it helps in our finding of the hit and run driver."

Jake's gaze had been steady on me, like he was thinking deeply about something before he responded, but finally whatever he was wrestling with in his mind had a winner. "We gave the footage already to the cops. As a matter of fact, they played the footage right here in this office the morning of the accident and I saw it and listened to them as they watched. I know that the vehicle that drove off had stolen plates. You still willing to shell out a C note given what I just told you."

"Yes. And I thank you for the honesty, but just because the cops think the footage is a bust, doesn't mean that it is. We have our own way of looking at data and got our own experts, maybe no better than the cops, but they are different and thus they might see something the cops missed, or vice versa, just cause they are different."

"Well," Jake said, "it's your C note. It'll take me a few minutes to make a copy of the DVD. Make yourself as much at home as a guy that don't drink can be in a place where it flows like a river."

Jake took his sweet time and I did what I always did when there wasn't anything else to do, I pulled out a book and read. It was a real screamer, it was about a detective that was a cross between Colombo and Monk, who caused the crook to confess, mostly by irritating him so much the guy would rather go to jail than to put up with the detective.

"Here she be," Jake eventually said and tossed me a DVD that I grabbed in mid-air. "Hope it helps, and I really hope I see you again, providing you are bringing yet more of those Jacksons."

"I hope so too," I said. "And thanks for the help and for the honesty. Guy in my line of work don't meet too many honest people."

"Guy in any line of work don't meet too many honest people, either," Jake replied as he walked me back through the dance floor and back out into the bright sunshine.

Marvin had already closed up by the time I made my car which I hated, since I was gonna throw another twenty his way, just out of the goodness of my client's heart. But there was nothing except a couple of other cars that hadn't left for the night. I got into my car, checked my watch and then I saw Jake open the door and look my way. He waved and I waved back. Nice guy and all that. Then I pulled out of the parking lot and headed back to the office.

Once at the office I went to see Johnathan our ace data guy and I do mean ace. He could torture the data enough to make it scream which often helped if you were trying to show a connection between things that really weren't connected, but it helped our client if we showed a connection anyway. Statistics were wonderful that way, you could show correlation and right away people think you've showed causation.

Johnathan was just getting ready to go home and wasn't overjoyed to see me, but then again, Johnathan was very seldom overjoyed about anything. "Roche," he said. "It'll wait till tomorrow. Go home, pretend you've got a life outside of this place just like the rest of us pretend."

"It will wait," I said, "but unless you're busy, I need you to see if you can find out who if anyone a guy named Randolph Butree hanged with. The skip trace report has his address and SSN and a lot of other things. He was killed in a car crash on the fifteenth and me and Bug are trying to find out all we can about him to keep our client out of the pokey. What I really need to know is, where did he hang, who did he hang with and if he was a sot or a junkie. But I'll take anything you can toss my way."

"I'll toss it like a salad tomorrow," Johnathan said. "Now go away from my desk like a good little detective." And I went away from his desk and went home and pretended I had a life. I also dropped the DVD in the in basket of the audio visual people, and they too had gone home already, so any questions I had for them would have to wait until the morrow.

STARKEY THE FINANCIAL MAN

Starkey had gotten up from his sleepless night grouchy, but then he was often grouchy and sleep had little or nothing to do with it. Being fifty and broke was a more logical reason.

Starkey called up his go-to financial guy, a big time jerk but still on the company payroll and would supply you with some financial info if it pleased him to do so. Starkey sighed and dialled the phone number.

"This is Melvin," a less than melodic voice said over the phone.

"This is Starkey," Starkey replied. "I need to know everything there is to know about United Transhipment, or at least everything you are willing to tell me, that is already covered by National's contract with your firm."

"In other words you are not going to buy me a reasonably priced meal to get the information quickly, as a civilised man would do," Melvin said.

"Not this time," Starkey said. "Partially because what you called reasonably priced, ain't, and because I ain't civilised, but mostly because United Transhipment is footing the bill for this and I don't want them to know I was checking them out."

"I will send a well written report in about a week," Melvin said.

"Fine, but now that you've got an excuse to write a report, I just need the highlights. I promise the next time I get a case where I can expense a reasonably priced meal, you will be invited to feast to your heart's desire."

"I doubt your veracity, but one must trust his fellow man upon occasion," Melvin sniffed. "Off the top of my head, I would say you have a fairly nasty corporate customer on your hands. The rumours are that they are just a front for the laundering of all sorts of bad money, and the rumours are likely true. They also do legit work, as they have to do legit work, that is as cover for what they really make their money on. Good luck with them, Stark, and don't worry, I'll attend your funeral, even if you are the cheapest detective I've ever known."

The information did not surprise Starkey as he knew from the gitgo the guys were shady. After all, they had gotten his name from a shady doctor he'd tried to put in the slammer. While the doctor avoided jail time, Starkey had revealed his illegal insider trading on a short sale and had cost the doctor a million or two. Doubtless the doc could afford it, but it didn't seem he would be willing to refer Starkey to anyone unless in the referring Starkey would somehow get skewered.

Starkey hung up the phone and then called Thompson to report what he had found and to have him let corporate know there was a report coming from Melvin's firm. Then he told Thompson his plans for that night.

Thompson growled and said he would send back-up as it was a minimum two-man and possibly a two-car job for what Starkey had in mind. Starkey didn't want anyone with him, had never liked nor wanted a partner and he stood his ground.

"It's you neck," Thompson growled. "So watch it and call ever couple of hours."

"Sure," Starkey lied. "Glad to."

THE TAO OF TAILING

Starkey was at the parking lot across from Smittee's at 8:30 p.m. Luckily this parking lot was free after five since street parking was also free after five, and as a result the lot was empty after five. There were a few cars that parked there for a few minutes to go into the liquor store on the corner, but none stayed for longer than five minutes. That suited Starkey right to the ground.

Surveillance is about the worst job a rent-a-cop has to do. Usually it's long, boring, and requires vigilance, and those three things are counter to each other. It is hard to pay attention on anything that isn't fun for more than a few minutes, and believe me watching sober people enter a bar and drunk people leave a bar isn't fun.

Starkey had the latest gizmo from the National Agency, night vision glasses that had been left over from Operation Desert Storm and bought at the military surplus store. Regardless of its origin and the fact it was over twenty years old, it still did the trick and Starkey had no problem picking out the faces of those who entered and left the bar.

Around 9 p.m. he spotted Bigg. Bigg stopped for a moment to send his cigarette flying into the night, making a visible arc that was doubtless pleasant to see in real light but was irritating to Starkey with his night vision glasses. But at least his prey had showed this night, Starkey had worried that he wouldn't and since skip trace had not yet found his address, Starkey would've been stuck.

Starkey was trailing Bigg because he felt Bigg was the easiest to trace. Himley might have been a better one but he seemed to be more of the brains than Bigg and for sure not Wreek. Wreek, regardless of how close his name came to Wreck, was a driver and those guys could not only drive, but they were usually hard to tail, as they always took great pride in their ability to both spot and lose a tail. So Bigg was the guy, plus Bigg was the muscle, which meant he was likely to be the one to confront anyone that might be interfering with whatever skulduggery these guys were up to.

Bigg seemed to take his own sweet time in the bar and to make that sweet time go by, Starkey tried counting cars and also tried to see if he could make out the occupants of those cars as they sped by. It was useless, as the glasses weren't that good, and looking at people whizzing by wasn't any more fun than watching them enter and exit a bar, so Starkey gave it up as a lost cause and just went back to thinking.

He had thought there was something amiss with the so-called poker crew almost from the minute he had entered the bar and braced Sacks the bartender. Typically, the bartender will be more than glad to take a buck or two from you for information, but they don't seem to think overly long on the subject. Sacks had seemed to not only hesitate but to think on the subject before he had agreed to talk. Starkey thought that Sacks was weighing his options and felt that there were too many patrons at the bar that had seen Garson, whom they knew as Lenny, that he couldn't rightly get away with denying he had seen him.

Given that, Sacks had agreed to set up the meeting with Himley and Starkey would have bet dollars to donuts that he had tried to call Himley but hadn't gotten through. That was why he announced loudly when Starkey had met Himley that Starkey was a private copper.

Himley realised right away that the only way to throw the private cop off whatever scent that was at issue was to feed him the song and dance about the poker room. Then he got together with his partners and set up the meeting to assure Starkey that they just played poker for fun and that this Lenny was no more than a casual acquaintance.

Starkey hoped he hadn't given away his non-belief in their so-called story but the fact that Wreek had tailed him meant they were at least suspicious of him. The thought that they too were searching for Garson had crossed his mind and since Garson was an expert money launderer then it was likely he had taken money from them to launder and had laundered it all the way into his own bank account. Thus Wreek was trying to find out where Starkey lived so that he could trail Starkey and if Starkey found Garson, Wreek would be there to snatch Garson from him.

Of course, it all might be in his head and that Garson really did go there to play card games and drink a few shots, and that Wreek just happened to be heading the same way he was when Starkey spotted him. It was also possible that the Government only has your best interest in mind when they make policy. Anything is possible.

After what seemed a thousand years but was only a little over an hour, Bigg came back out of the bar, with Himley walking beside him. The two of them walked a few feet away from the door of Smittee's and then began to talk. Whatever they were saying, they didn't want anyone else to hear, for they looked up and down the street constantly.

At the end of the conversation, Bigg nodded his head and then snapped a salute and clicked his heals together like he was signalling his understanding of an order. Himley openly laughed, and then the two parted, with Himley heading back into the bar.

Bigg walked into the parking lot and in a few moments a Chevy Malibu pulled out. Starkey couldn't see the driver but hoped it was Bigg as he cranked up and lit out after him.

There are times when shadowing a subject isn't all that hard, and that's typically in daylight, on streets you know and with a partner you can work with to keep the guy from seeing you to many times. But this was at night, in a car and Starkey was alone, so it wasn't the easiest shadowing he had ever done. And while Starkey wasn't a world class shadower, he knew guys that could follow a snowflake in a blizzard, he was adequate and he managed to keep the Malibu in sight and hoped he wasn't seen in the process.

After about ten minutes, the Malibu pulled into the parking lot of a dance club called Night of Colours. Since there was an attendant at the parking lot and since there was no way he could pull in without Bigg likely seeing him, he chose instead to drive on and then around the block. He finally found a spot just down the street from the night club which let him see the parking lot exit without being to conspicuous himself, and he parked there to await Bigg's exit if the Malibu belonged to Bigg and luckily it did.

Bigg seemed to either not like the club or the club didn't like him because he was out of the building just about as soon as Starkey had found his parking spot. A large man had walked out with Bigg and was walking with him to the parking lot. The two were talking but there didn't seem to be much hand movement, which usually meant they didn't know each other that well but they weren't angry at each other, at least not actively angry.

Once they reached Bigg's car and Bigg got in to leave, Starkey saw the large man shrug his shoulders in the classic, got me, style, so that meant he didn't know or didn't want to reveal whatever Bigg wanted to know. Starkey couldn't tell Bigg's face at that distance but he imagined it was not the happiest of faces.

Bigg pulled away from the man and left the parking lot with Starkey in close but reasonable pursuit. Bigg drove straight for the interstate and hit it. At this time of night there wasn't much traffic and he was cruising at 80 mph quickly and Starkey too was cruising at 80 mph but he wasn't happy doing so. Starkey didn't want a cop pulling him over and he knew the company wouldn't pay for it, regardless of whether he was on a tail or not.

After about forty minutes and after the city lights and even the suburb lights had dimmed appreciably, Bigg took exit 85 and was on a four-lane highway that was just in the suburbs. Starkey pulled up his search a little and fell back, hoping he didn't lose Bigg, but shadowing is a game for a crowd and not for two. He would rather lose Bigg than risk Bigg seeing him. Starkey could always pick up Bigg another night and now that he had the tag number, he could get AV to hack into the city cameras to help him locate Bigg for another tail.

Bigg stopped at a supermarket, one of the standard type that one sees in most cities and suburbs. This was a fairly safe place for Starkey to park, since it was one of those open till midnight places and there were still several cars around the lot, so Starkey pulled into a place close but not too close to Bigg.

Bigg spent about fifteen minutes in the store, typical guy time, get in, get it, get out, and walked out with two bags of groceries. All that Starkey could see was the top of a bottle protruding that might have been wine or vinegar but Starkey would bet it was something a might stronger.

Bigg got back into his car and spent a couple of minutes arranging the groceries. If he was checking to see if he was being tailed, he was excellent at doing so without being seen. Starkey was as alert as a private cop can because, if Bigg made him and came over, Starkey sure as hell wasn't gonna be there.

But all seemed well as Bigg cranked his car and pulled out of the parking lot. Starkey gave it a few seconds then he followed again, well aware that if Bigg had spotted him, that he was likely being lead to the slaughter.

As Bigg drove and Starkey followed, the suburb traffic began to die down and the four-lane road turned into a two-lane road. After about ten minutes, Starkey fell way back and followed Bigg's car lights as best he could. Luckily Bigg was staying on the one road and that made the trailing somewhat easier.

After what seemed an eternity to Starkey, Bigg pulled off to the right onto another but much smaller two-lane road. Starkey drove right on past the turn off, since it would be a possible give away if he turned right where Bigg had turned, right after Bigg had turned. Starkey went down the streets for another half mile, spotted a service station that was closed, and he pulled into the service station and turned around and headed back towards the turn off.

Tipton Road, if it mattered, was the name of the two-lane road where Bigg had turned onto. Starkey followed that road and hoped he would spot Bigg's Malibu, even though it was pitch black. There were no houses for the first half mile, just pasture on either side, but finally Starkey came upon a trailer where sure enough the outside security light showed that Bigg's car was parked, along with another car, a Caddy from the look of it. Starkey wanted the plate number bad for that Caddy but the light was too dim and he sure as hell wasn't gonna try to sneak over to it since he might not be tangling only with Bigg but with two people. Starkey knew that Bigg wouldn't need no whole lot of help to stomp a fat and fifty guy into the ground.

The only other thing that Starkey noted was small plastic deer that was posed as if it were grazing on the gravel of the driveway. Redneck chic.

Starkey pulled on by the trailer looking for someplace to park where he could keep an eye on the place, at least for a few minutes. He wanted to call HQ and give them his GPS data so they could see who owned the trailer and thus add more burden to skip trace, since it was sure Bigg didn't own it or they would have turned his name up on their last data search. He also hoped the Caddy would leave and he could follow.

About three hundred yards beyond the trailer, there was a road that lead to one of the pastures. Starkey doused his lights and then backed into that road, it allowed him to see the trailer as he talked with the night guy at HQ. With a quick push of a button, Starkey called the night desk and got McGee who was the lucky stiff on night duty.

"Hey, McGee," Starkey said. "I need to find out who owns a trailer on 240 Tipton Road, and it's either Mason or Jefferson county, I don't think I crossed a county line but I may have."

"Hey yourself, Starkey," McGee said. "I'll leave it for the data guys. You having fun earning all this overtime."

"I wouldn't describe it as fun, but the overtime helps," Starkey replied, and just as he was about to hang up the phone, he heard a loud blast, followed by another loud blast. The blast sound rang through the copse of trees that surrounded Starkey, bouncing and echoing so that it was impossible to tell where it came from. He slammed his body against the bench seat of his car, at least as best he could. The rational part of his mind was telling him that the blasts, which sounded like a shotgun blast, had not been meant for him or else he would already be dead, but the irrational part of his brain, and likely the part that has ensured the preservation of the human species said, get low and get down and do it fast.

Starkey held his position on the seat for a full minute and maybe longer, then after no more shots rang out, he popped back up. He carefully listened to the silence, and silence it still was as the crickets and other night creatures had not yet taken up their night songs. They to, it seemed, did not care for strange noises in the night.

Starkey finally remembered his phone was still on, but the connection had been broken when he made the dive into his car seat, which was unfortunate, because that meant the shotgun blasts were not recorded. Starkey continued to be still and not make any sound and definitely did not crank his engine. Of course, the blasts could just be a hunter somewhere close by, but one gets suspicious when one is on a tail job and that's how one survives.

Eventually, as regardless of how much you don't want to have to do something that must be done, Starkey opened his door. He was able to push in the light button on the door so that the overhead light didn't come on. Then he cautiously walked up the dark road towards the overhead safety light. He kept to the shadows as much as possible and the night was dark so the possibility of them spotting him was slim, and since the crickets had started their nightly complaining, the chances of being heard was lessened as well.

Within about a hundred yards of the trailer, Starkey knew he didn't have to worry about Bigg hearing him, cause Bigg wasn't gonna hear anything else on this green earth ever again. He lay in the doorway of his trailer, half his body sloped down towards the ground and the rest just barely in the trailer. Even from 100 yards Starkey could see the blood, and more impressively, the blood splatter on the trailer. It was a dark blotch against the white siding and did not look a bit red in this light.

The Caddy was gone, and Starkey hoped the driver and all beings associated with the Caddy were gone as well. There didn't seem to be anyone else about, or if they were they were hiding. Starkey had taken worse chances in his day, so he walked up into the light and over to the body. He'd seen death a few times in his career and he thought the man was dead, still, he reached down and tried to feel the pulse at the carotid artery on the neck. There was none, and Starkey had put on gloves so that he didn't leave any prints. At least he felt he had done the best he could for a fellow man, even if that fellow man would likely have shot him if he had gotten the chance.

With a grimace, Starkey pushed is phone back on and dialled 911. "There has been a shooting at 240 Tipton Road. I'm unsure of the county I'm in. Yes, I'll wait for the police and the ambulance, although I think the man is dead. My name is Joe Starkey."

Starkey waited far away from the dead body, but he waited. Private cop 101 is don't ever leave a homicide scene unless there's no way to tie you back to that scene. Starkey didn't think he could be tied back, but since there wasn't any way someone could pin it on him, he thought it best to call it in and see where it went. He would rather it be city cops as county cops, but a lifetime of disappointment had demonstrated quite conclusively that you don't generally get your rathers.

The cops got there within ten minutes, which wasn't surprising since it was well past midnight and there wasn't much in the way of night life this far out from the city. The locals would be looking mostly for speeders and drunk drivers and would already be out and about and thus quicker to the scene. There were two of them, one big, one small, one male, one female, neither looked too thrilled to see Starkey.

"You Joe Starkey?" the female cop asked as she got out of the driver's side of the car.

"Guilty," Starkey replied and tried to fake a smile without success.

The female cop and the male cop walked over to the corpse and they too tried the neck pulse with the same results. The male went to the trunk of the police car and began to pull out barriers and the ever-present yellow tape. Starkey wondered how police work ever got done before the invention of yellow tape.

The cops did what they always do, block off areas, make sure that the scene stays as clean as possible and generally make a nuisance of themselves. Starkey stayed well away, knowing they would get to him soon enough and he doubted if it would be pleasant.

A second police car pulled up and behind him was a blaring ambulance whose sound was especially eerie given how quiet the night had been only moments before. An aged cop, probably the local chief of whatever hamlet this trailer was residing in, got out of the second police car and said hello to everyone, and called them all by first name, including the two ambulance people. Then he walked over towards Starkey and even though the man looked harmless enough, Starkey was wary.

"You Joe Starkey?" the aged cop said in a gravelly voice that fit both his face and his occupation.

"Yeah."

The old cop thrust out his hand and said, "Jack Torrence, I'm the police chief of Pine City. Just happens this trailer falls within our jurisdiction and not the county's. Politics and land taxes account for that, cause logic sure can't." The old cop said this with a smile. Starkey didn't see the humour but smiled back anyway.

"Give me the nickel ride, then we can get you back to HQ for a formal statement," Torrence said. "I understand you're a private cop."

"Yes," Starkey said. "I don't know how much I can add to what is visible to the plain eye. But I was trailing the deceased, his name is Jackson Jones but he goes by Bigg. I have interest in him as he may connect with another case I'm on. I know from our own resources that Bigg had been in prison up till about five years ago. I assume you know much more or will, since your reports will likely be more accurate than ours. I trailed him from a bar in the city called Smittee's, and the reason I had to trail him was our report had no known address for him. I saw a Caddy parked here when I passed by, that was about an hour ago now. I passed the place on by to find a spot where the trailer was still visible to park and call my HQ as well as keep an eye on Bigg. I found a spot and I parked at a small tractor road just on down that two-lane a few hundred yards." Starkey stopped talking long enough to gesture towards where his car was parked.

"I pulled in and would likely have spent just a few minutes there while I called my HQ to see if we could find out who owned this trailer or this piece of land the trailer is on. I was then gonna quietly slip back to the city. But before I could leave I heard two shotgun blasts. I hid as best I could in the front seat of my car for a couple of minutes, and then after no more blasts, I creeped up here to see what I could see. The Caddy had already gone, and Bigg was deader than a door nail."

"Touch anything?" Torrence asked.

"Nothing except the neck of yon dead crook," Starkey said. "And I wore a glove when I did that. I thought he looked dead, but you never know and if I had felt a pulse I would have at least covered him with a blanket or something to try to preserve his life till the ambulance got here. But he was beyond blankets, way beyond."

"Never get used to 'em," Torrence said as his eyes went to the body. "Dead bodies, I mean. Mostly I only see 'em at car accidents, we don't get a murder here but once in a blue moon. I know of nothing worse than a shotgun blast. A blast sends the blood a flying and it chews up the body worse than most car accidents." Torrence shifted his eyes directly to Starkey and asked, "Don't suppose you're gonna tell me why you were trailing Bigg, are you. Most of you private coppers seem to think you are a doctor or lawyer or some such and have privilege, which you ain't got by the way."

"I'm like most private coppers in one way. I ain't gonna tell you squat unless my lawyers sign off on it first." Starkey reached into his billfold and pulled out Gonzo's card—the National Detective Agency lawyer who was always the first one to talk with the cops, and that was always unless you didn't want to keep your job at National. "Call Mr Gonzales there," Starkey said. "After he and I have a chat, he'll tell you and me what I can or can't say."

Torrence took the card. "We'll talk more on this after you've made a proper report and signed off on it. I'll let you talk to your attorney after that, since I ain't gonna charge you until after I read your report."

"I've got twenty years under my belt as a private copper," Starkey said. "I know I don't have to say squat or sign squat until I see a lawyer if I ask for one. You know it too. Don't make a difficult time worse."

Torrence just smiled again, showing teeth that needed bushing and bridgework badly and if Starkey could tell that in the dim light of the safety bulb, then it must look a fright in daylight.

"Well," Torrence replied. "You never know what a guy does and don't know until you try him. Let's be friends instead."

"Let's," Sharkey said, but there was not a whole lot of enthusiasm in the saying.

"Notice anything about the Caddy that could help nail the bastard?" Torrence asked. "Like the tag number?"

"I would have already told you if I had," Sharkey replied. "It was too dark to see much and I won't even swear it was a Caddy SUV but it looked it, or at least looked it as much as a quick glance while driving by at night with a lousy safety light being the only illumination it could look like."

"I got it," Torrence said. "It was damn dark and you weren't overly interested. Well, we'll see if we can find any Caddy SUV's on our street cams between midnight and ..." Torrence stopped and looked at his watch and said, "2 a.m."

"You through with me? I'd like to get some shut eye and consult with my attorney before I make a formal statement."

"Don't doubt it," Torrence replied. "By the way, just for the record, I don't care. We'll discuss things and by all means call your lawyer, but you are now a material witness in a murder case and you ain't going anywhere."

Starkey assumed as much but at least there was some satisfaction in this otherwise dismal affair. He would get to wake Gonzo at 2 a.m. and given his relationship with Gonzo that was somewhat satisfying.

AV PEOPLE ARE JUST PEOPLE TOO, PROBABLY

I had a couple of things to do and the first was to stop by the AV room with the DVD that Jake from the Night of Colours had given me. I saw Roomey who we called Runty behind his back cause he was small, but he had the personality of an alligator, so it was best not to call him Runty to his face.

Roomey could take any old DVD or video tape and expose more secrets than the worst politician has in his closet, so he was a much needed and much sought out asset of National Detective but the trouble is you had to work with him to get those secrets. As a result, he was the most praised man at National to his face and the most cursed behind his back, which proves one point—as long as your help outweighs your hurt, you won't get fired.

"Roomey old buddy," I said and he looked up from some piece of equipment that I did not recognise and before I could go further he exploded, "Roach, I got real work here. You know the system, log it, provide the who, what, why and tell me anything to look for. You don't just drop a DVD in my in box and assume magic will happen. Other than that, go away."

"You're gonna hurt my feelings one day," I said and Roomey smiled at the thought. It seemed a compliment today wasn't gonna allow me to jump line, so I just said, "Thanks for being such a joy to work with," and I reached for the log book and the sheet I had to complete in order to get the work.

I left Roomey doing whatever it was that he did and went over to skip trace to see how Jonathan was getting along on my request for known associates of Butree. Johnathan waved at me as I walked in. "You have luck and you also have another partner."

"I'm glad about the luck, but I didn't know they had fired Bug, though it wouldn't surprise me if they did," I said and from behind me I heard Bug say "I heard that," as I knew he would since I had seen him come in out of the corner of my eye.

"That's not what I meant," Johnathan said. "It seems that the known associates of Mr Randolph Butree include the name of several men that Starkey asked for information on. And to top that, one of the men was killed last night, and Starkey is being held as a material witness."

"Looks like none of your partners have any luck," Bug said and I saw him pass a wink to Johnathan.

"Names and details, Johnathan old boy," I said.

"The dead man is one Bigg Jones, used to be hired muscle for anybody that wasn't overly concerned with finesse on a job. He or maybe I should say, it, as I'm not all that certain that Bigg is human, got out of the joint about five years ago. Starkey called in last night, or I guess really this morning, to tell us that this guy Bigg had been shotgunned to death. From what I heard, Starkey had to get Gonzo out of bed cause the local police chief was yanking his chain."

"Poor Starkey," Bug said. "So far from heaven, so close to Gonzo."

"There were two other names that I found," Johnathan continued, "that were both on Butree's list and on Starkey's. There is a guy named Tom Wreek, who's relatively new but rumour has it, and this is police rumour so it's true, that he has been a driver on a few jobs that required iron nerves. Starkey reported that he was followed by Wreek after making himself known at a bar called Smittee's. Starkey thought highly of Wreek's skills, which may or may not mean anything, cause all you guys think you are an expert when you spot a tail, but you can't really do statistics that way, since you never know how many times you didn't spot a tail."

"The man's a statistical genius," Bug said to me. "I feel humbled to be in his presence."

Johnathan guffawed which meant the joke wasn't that funny, even though I thought it was, and that he was above such petty things. I nodded at Johnathan because, unlike Bug, I did care that Johnathan worked on my things and not throw them to the bottom of the list, like he did anything Bug asked of him.

"The final guy's name is Bart Himley. He runs a locksmith shop over on third avenue," Johnathan said. "It seems these guys play poker together, and it also seems these guys were thought to be involved in the First National robbery from a few weeks ago. Of course, the cops think a lot of guys are good for that robbery, and these guys, and particularly Himley who has no priors that I can find nor any rumours associated with his name, may not be involved. However, with the deaths of two of the people in the foursome, and with one being an expert at getting around electronic security and the other an expert of making sure once that security has been gotten around that no security guard was gonna cause any trouble, then I'd bet a whole month's salary the cops are gonna pick up the other two for questioning."

"No bet," I said. "Anything else that horrid but useful brain of yours has come up with?"

"Starkey's latest report shows that he trailed Bigg to a nightclub called Night of Colours. There was a wreck at the intersection in front of Night of Colours on the fifteenth." Johnathan was rather proud of this bit of information and he added, "My horrid but much more than useful brain has deduced that you might find that of interest, since you asked for the wrecks in the city on the fifteenth. Can't draw any conclusions statistically, of course, from one piece of data, but I do think it's what you detectives call a clue."

"What's the clue part of that?" Bug asked.

"Well," Johnathan answered, "maybe the hit and run driver was coming out of the parking lot of the dance club. Just a thought."

"Thanks but I'm not sure it's not just coincidence," I said. "Runty is running the DVD showing the wreck, a DVD by the way that was provided to me by the club, so if there is a connection, it doesn't necessarily mean the club is involved."

"I just do data analysis," Johnathan said. "I leave the detecting to you, but I know the cops already have the DVD footage since they would automatically ask for any camera footage that looked promising. Since the club had already given the cops the footage, I don't think they cared that they gave it to you. After all, anybody with any experience with the law in this town knows you can buy about anything you need from the cops."

There was something in that so I nodded and said, "Maybe," since I didn't want Johnathan to get a much bigger head than he already had, if that were even possible.

I headed towards the dispatcher, and he saw me coming and gave me the automatic don't bother me look, but I bothered him anyway.

"Need to talk to Starkey," I said. "Where is he?"

"He and Gonzo are on their way back from beautiful Pine City where they just had a delightful time with the police, at least that's what I sort of interpreted between the curses," the dispatcher said. "Arrival in about forty-five minutes I'd say."

"Let Starkey know to come by my office," I told him.

"I'll make the request," he said dismissively. "But you guys do what you want anyway, so if Starkey don't show up, take it up with him."

I left Mr Cheerful and headed back to my desk, stopping along the way to find a bad but free cup of coffee. Bug was already at his desk looking at a skip trace report.

"Anything to note?" I asked.

"The accident in front of the Night of Colours was probably the fault of the geezer that got killed, it seems not only was he up late he was also high as a kite. The guy's name was Travers, and he'd seen more than his share of the inside of the drunk tank. Per the police report, the other car, the one that ran away was just coming through the green light, and they were only going about 20 mph when they get slammed by the BMW going at least 60. No way the hit and run car was gonna be found at fault. So why did they run, if they were the one hit?"

"Maybe they had $4 million in the car and would rather not explain where that kinda money came from to the police," I ventured.

"Yeah, that kinda occurred to me too," Bug said. "And if Butree got killed there, then guess what, they couldn't just dump the body and run. That still doesn't explain why they had to set up Cready in a fake accident, but it does get us a little closer."

"That it does," I agreed. "Come on, Bug, I'll buy you a decent cup of coffee to celebrate."

Bug nodded and followed me over to the office coffee pot and I poured him a cup of our brew. He didn't seem impressed.

Just then I saw Starkey and Gonzo walk into the lobby, and I've known Starkey for a long time and I've never seen him look worse.

"Got time for a quick meeting?" I asked as he strolled past my desk. "It may be we're working the same case."

"Yeah?" Starkey asked, "How so?"

"Let's go into room number one. Gonzo, can you see if Runty will bring in the DVD I gave him to play for us. Tell him it doesn't have to be processed," I said.

"Damn Roach," Gonzo said. "I hate facing Runty even with a decent night sleep and decent coffee in me."

"He'll more listen to you than me," I said.

"Okay, but you know there was a time I was a real lawyer," Gonzo replied and then he ambled off towards Runty's area.

"Rough night?" Bug asked and Starkey gave him the don't get me started look.

"You know," Starkey said, "some guys shouldn't be cops and I just met a whole bunch of them. They seem to think that acting tough and threatening me with jail and violence and just by being jerks that I could somehow talk to them without legal representation. I do wish they would take some sensitivity training ever now and again."

"Well," I said, "I do feel your pain having been the guests of the boys in blue a few times myself but we need to get you caught up. It seems the guy that you tailed last night is tied in with our case, at least as a known associate. Also you trailed the guy to Night of Colours and it is highly likely that the wreck that happened there on the fifteenth is also related to our case. As I understand it you are looking for a missing person; we on the other hand are trying to find out if an accident was real or faked. Good money would have said it was real, but now I'm not so sure."

"There are several guys," Starkey said, "That seemed to be in cahoots over something. I am pretty sure it's the bank job but then again I'm not certain it's the bank job, but I am certain they are lying to me, and usually where there's a lie there's a reason for the lie."

Starkey gave them the info he'd gathered at Smittee's and I passed along what we had gathered in our search for Butree. Just as I finished talking, Runty walked in and handed me the DVD. "I haven't had any time to process, but I made a copy and will get on it ASAP. Gonzo said it was important."

I didn't know when it mattered what Gonzo said, but I took the DVD readily and put it in the player in the meeting room. Bug said, "Roomey, I take back the last three things I've said about you."

"Sure, Bug," was all Runty answered and he left us to go do whatever else someone else asked, and I was pretty sure we fell back to the bottom of the list.

"Bug," I said, "I don't mind you irritating Runty on your own cases, but mine are difficult enough without adding lack of AV help to the list."

"You guys don't understand psychology," said Bug who had not even made it through one semester of college. "Runty likes being kidded."

"Yeah, just about as much as I liked Chief Jack Torrence of the Pine City Police Department," Starkey replied.

I put the DVD into the player and Bug hit the lights. The accident unfolded before our eyes. We saw the SUV pull out of the Night of Colours club parking lot, going slowly and just hitting the green light, which wasn't all that hard since there wasn't much traffic at 5.08 in the a.m. Then the BMW came into view for just a section and smacked the SUV seven ways from Sunday.

There was no sound but the crash still startled me for a second. There was a lot of force in that smack and it was obvious that the BMW driver was deader than hell as the BMW, even though it was the one providing the force, just folded like a cheap chair. A large man jumped out of the passenger's side of the SUV and looked at the damage done to the side of the vehicle. He seemed to be shouting something. Then the driver of the SUV got out and came around, he wasn't as big but still he wasn't small.

The SUV had a badly dented side, but the vehicle otherwise looked okay. The BMW however had smacked and recoiled and folded as it got out of the way. Neither of the men went over to check the BMW, but the driver did look quickly to make sure there was no debris in front of the SUV. The far side passenger door opened and a small man hopped out and talked rapidly. Then all three of them jumped back into the SUV and it left, making good speed.

All of this happened during a driving rain storm and the video quality wasn't all that good, still, I thought it might be good enough for Starkey to pick out Bigg or one of the others. So as I ran the accident again I asked, "You recognise any of them, Starkey?"

"Not that I would testify to," he said. "The three have the general size and shape of the three men I met at Smittee's, that is Bigg, Himley and Wreek. I'd bet they're the same men, but I couldn't testify conclusively that they are."

"I'll get the plates on the hit and run over to skip trace," Bug said, "but without doubt they were stolen."

"I agree," I said. "But we always look into the obvious. Well, Starkey ole buddy, seems like our cases are sorta kinda related. How you want to go from here?"

"One of you could go to Smittee's and act like a right old drunk for a night or so and see if you can pick up something. You might even try to tail Wreek or Himley and see if that leads somewhere."

"I don't know," I said. "If I was Wreek and or Himley I would be hard to find as the cops probably want to talk with them and it seems somebody might be after them. Of course, Bigg was a hard man in a hard business, and it is just possible that he got killed for something unrelated to either of our cases."

"True," Starkey said. "But I still think somebody should just go and hang out for a night and see if they can hear anything useful."

"And I had a wild thought," I said. "Someone needs to go to the Night of Colours and hang about. There's likely nothing on the surface there, but you might see something that would help. That person can also look over the head of security there, one Jake Rothlein. I don't know if he's involved, but he went out of his way to be friendly to me and that always makes me suspicious."

Johnathan walked in. "The owner of 240 Tipton is an entity called Dublet Holdings. The group actually own several hundred acres out there and rent most of it out to local farmers for grazing and farming. Guess who owns Dublet Holdings?"

Starkey said, "United Transhipment."

"Give the man a cigar," Johnathan said. "And give him a bath while you are at it." With that Johnathan walked out and we three real detectives stared at each other for a while.

"You know," I said, "it might be interesting to see who owns Night of Colours. And it might be interesting to pull a skip trace on Jake Rothstein, the friendly guy that just wanted to help."

"I'll get over to skip trace and get them started," Starkey said. "And then I will go home, even if Wreek is following me, and I will sleep the day away. The only question that remains is who is gonna go to Smittee's and who is gonna go to Night of Colours."

"They got naked dancers at the Night of Colours?" Bug asked.

"Don't know," Starkey answered truthfully. "I've been to Smittee's however and they definitely do not have naked dancers there."

"Dibbs on Night of Colours," Bug said and looked menacingly at me.

"What the hell," I said. "One den of iniquity is equivalent to another. I'll take Smittee's."

Starkey got up to leave and said, "I think I'll shadow one Jake Rothstein tonight. If you see me, Bug, give me wide berth."

"Like I'd want to be seen with you," Bug sniffed.

With that our impromptu meeting ended and we went our separate ways.

WHERE NOBODY KNOWS YOUR NAME

I got to Smittee's around 8 p.m. It seemed to be doing less than stellar business, and after I had a drop of their best scotch, I knew why. It was lucky I asked for it straight, cause if I had asked for it with water, there wouldn't even have been a touch of scotch in it. Besides the watered down scotch, the place looked like most bars, I suppose. Not being a connoisseur of the night life as was Starkey, all bars looked pretty much the same to me.

I grabbed a seat at a table that looked like it had seen better days, filled with cigarette burns and wobbly. Well, I wasn't there for the ambiance. I settled as comfortably as I could in the straight back chair and decided this place wasn't built for comfort, which was odd as I would think a bar would want to keep you there as long as you had money to spend.

The bartender, Sacks was his name per Starkey, looked over my way every now and then, and a few of the regulars looked at me with the eyes that said, this guy don't belong. But nobody shouted at me to leave, and much more importantly nobody shot at me.

I had brought a flask and when I was sure no one was looking, I poured my drink into the flask. Then I ordered another. I kept this up through four doubles over about an hour and a half and after that, since I didn't talk to anyone or bother anyone, I just became background and no one looked at me, except for Sacks, as he would make the rounds every half hour or so.

Things started to get interesting about 10 p.m. I saw several young men come in and with a wave at Sacks, head back to one of the rooms in the rear. They were only there for a few minutes and then they were off again. This stayed steady for the rest of the two hours that I felt I could safely stay at the bar.

It was obvious to me that there was some sort of gambling going on, likely it was the numbers game. Even though the numbers racket now has a lot of competition from the state lottery, it still thrives and it particularly thrives in poor areas of town, and a lot of the young men I had seen were minorities. The truth is, the numbers game provides a better return on investment, if that's the correct term for a game that only suckers play, but the house only takes about twenty per cent in a numbers racket and the state and fed usually takes fifty per cent of the lottery winnings in taxes. Even people dumb enough to gamble at the odds provided by the lottery can do that math. It's true that the numbers game doesn't bring in nearly as much as it once had, since the lottery definitely cut into the take. The wealthy no longer had to give their money to unsavoury characters to gamble, but the poor people still bet a lot of their hard earned on the numbers racket, and there are a lot more poor people than wealthy people.

I used my miniature camera that I kept in my right pocket to take some shots of the lads and of Sacks. I wanted to ask Sully how big the fix was in for this place, since it was obvious the young men weren't overly concerned at being seen coming and going. The cops had to know it was here, and that meant the cops were either bought off, or thought it not worth the bother. Sully would know which, for fifty bucks of course.

I got up from my chair, weaved about a second as if I was drunk, then I said, "Mind calling me a cab?" I said it loudly to be heard over the din.

Sacks nodded, and I think looked relieved. That made me look like an ordinary drunk and that was something he could live with.

After the cab arrived, I made my way unsteadily to the vehicle and gave the driver the address of an apartment house we used for just that purpose, a traceable address that was close to the train and bus lines. Since I had no reason to think the taxi driver was not in with Sacks—since often the drivers would overcharge a drunk and give part of the proceeds back to the bar owner for getting him the drunk in the first place—I kept up my act as a tipsy, if not quite drunk patron of Smittee's.

The taxi driver dropped me in front of the apartment house, charged me ten bucks more than the meter said and I gave him a ten buck tip also. Then I swayed my way inside the common door of the apartment complex and made my way to the elevator bank. I punched the elevator for the fourth floor and as I got in the elevator I glanced and saw the taxi had not yet moved from the front of the building. Now I was certain that Sacks and the taxi driver wanted to make sure I was legit. Or it might have been a coincidence. You never know in this game and we are taught to be cautious, and even if not taught you would learn it quickly or you would find yourself in the hospital a lot more than you cared to be.

Once I got to the fourth floor, I walked to the stairwell and quickly went back down to the lobby. I exited the back door without being seen, or if I was seen the guy was a better tracker than I was. I walked over to the subway and took the line that put me the closest to Smittee's. Then I walked back to my car which was parked across the street from Smittee's, the same lot that Starkey had used and I cranked the car and headed to my own small apartment.

I hadn't learned a whole lot but I did get flask of watered down scotch out of the night, so it wasn't a total loss.

BUG'S NIGHT OUT

Bug had arrived at the Night of Colours early and eager. Seldom did Bug get a night out what with Agnes his cat needing him home at nights, and even less seldom did the company pay for it, and almost never did it involve ogling half-clad women.

He seated himself at a table in the back, not because that would help seeing the naked ladies, but because it was the best place to spot what, if anything, was going on.

After the meeting with Starkey, Bug and Roche had gotten with skip trace and had them provide pictures of Garson, Rothlein, Himley and Wreek. Bug wanted to be sure he could identify them if they showed up at the Night of Colours and Roche wanted to be sure he could spot them if they showed up at Smittee's. They had memorised the faces because neither wanted to be caught with the photos on them. That could be hazardous to your health in the wrong circumstances.

Just as Roche had done, Bug had brought a flask to pour in the extravagantly priced drinks that were sold at this night club. It was a good thing he had done so, since the drinks here cost twice as much as at Smittee's but they also had twice as much alcohol. Still Bug couldn't help himself, he had to sip some of each of the drinks that came along, he was only human after all, though Runty might have disputed that.

Jake Rothlein was all over the night club for the whole night, which was to be expected, and he seemed to be an effervescent character, laughing and talking with a lot of employees and regulars. Jake seemed to know that you don't have to act tough to be tough, and looking at him, Bug wouldn't want to face him, especially since Jake was twenty years younger and forty pounds lighter.

Bug followed Jake as much as possible without being too obvious. Bug mostly stared straight ahead at the near naked, and sometimes totally naked, ladies that were demonstrating their athletic ability on stage, but he was keeping Rothlein in view. It isn't easy, but you can look at one thing and observe another and you learn that skill quickly in Bug's chosen profession.

It was a good four hours into the night, and Bug was on his ninth drink when a tall, good looking, thin young man walked into the club. Bug recognised him right away as Tom Wreek, and he knew right away that he needed direction on whether to shadow him or not. He kept his eyes on Wreek as he walked through the tables and headed towards the back office where Bug had seen Jake go a few minutes earlier. At just that time Bug decided he needed to go to the restroom, which just happened to be on the far side of the room and located just beside the office of Jake Rothlein.

Bug got up and walked slowly, looking to the left and to the right to see if anyone was observing him. There didn't appear to be anyone remotely interested, and so he stopped right beside the door to the restroom and continued to watch the ladies undress as he tried to hear what was being said inside the office. He hoped that if anyone saw him, they would put it down to a lecher that wanted to get closer to the good stuff for just a few moments.

The background noise from the club was way too high for Bug to hear what was going on in the office, but without doubt there were shouts. There also seemed to be some sort of physical alteration as Bug thought he heard a desk bumping or a chair being thrown. It was all guesswork of course, and they may just both have an interest in interior decoration and Wreek and Rothlein were just moving furniture.

The door suddenly opened and Bug walked quickly away from where he was standing and back into the darkness of the building. He saw what looked like a bleeding Wreek walk out. Wreek said something that was obviously hostile just from the way he said it back over his shoulder and then continued on the way out of the night club.

Walking quickly, Bug followed Wreek out and grabbed his phone and called Starkey as he walked.

"Stark," Bug said. "Wreek just visited Jake Rothlein and is now making a beeline for his car. I'm tailing him."

"You're welcome to try," Starkey replied. "The guy is known as a driver and I'm sure he'll spot a tail better than the average crook."

"You ain't been tailed until you been tailed by Bug," Bug replied and hung up. He made it to his car quickly and actually got in his vehicle quicker than Wreek had made it to his car, since Wreek had arrived late and had parked much further back in the lot.

Bug went ahead and pulled out and then turned left and went through the green light. He immediately pulled into one of the parking spots that were easily available on the street at this time of the night. Bug doused his lights and hoped that Wreek came this way, because if he didn't he might have to eat crow the next time he saw Starkey.

Bug had guessed right, as Wreek came through the green light and headed straight down Fourth. Bug pulled out and got behind him, running without headlights, hoping that would hide him, and hoping he didn't see a cop that would pull him over.

Fortune was with Bug as he trailed Wreek for two blocks and then Wreek turned to his right. Bug went through the green light and went down to the next turn. He put his lights on, figuring that if he pulled in behind Wreek now, Wreek wouldn't necessarily spot him as a tail.

Wreek finally pulled into the parking station that was attached to a large apartment building. Since Bug figured it would require a pass of some sort to get into that parking station, he stayed on the street and parked down from the apartment building about a block. There was plenty of parking on the street this time of night and Bug had chosen to go further than he needed just in case someone was watching.

Bug pulled out his night goggles. He didn't know if he should go up and brace Wreek or just leave it alone for the time being. He had hoped Wreek would lead him somewhere besides his apartment, but it looked like his hope was like most hopes, unfulfilled. As Bug watched the building he saw a silver Caddy pull into one of the parking spots just across from the building. Another car pulled beyond the Caddy and kept coming Bug's way. Bug didn't even have to look to see it was Starkey, since he saw the guy getting out of the Caddy was Jake Reinlein.

Starkey kept on driving and didn't stop, circling the block before coming back into the spot just in front of Bug. Starkey got out of his car and went up to Bug's car. Starkey didn't worry about his interior light giving him away as Reinlein was already in the apartment building. Bug rolled the window down and smiled at Starkey. "Fireworks I think," Bug said.

Starkey nodded back and said, "You got a pistol?"

Bug nodded. "Company issued .38, I assume you got the same."

Starkey nodded. "You know, it's highly likely that we will get our tails shot off by one or both of those guys. You think we should chance it?"

"I think," Bug said, "that one or both of them will be dead before we reach the apartment. I know that if we don't go up there, we might miss out on catching one of them at a weak moment. The moment when they might spill the beans on what this caper is all about."

"Probably," Starkey replied. "But I ain't got forty pounds of protection around my gut. If they shoot me it'll hurt."

"Tell me about it later," Bug said. "Let's go make the company proud of us."

Bug jumped out of the car and he and Sharkey walked towards trouble; they were both too old to do much running. Bug shivered even though it was a warm night. Bravado was fine and had to be said between men when they were doing something dangerous, but that didn't mean they would do it with relish.

The two detectives walked into the apartment building and Bug said, "I got the elevator you got the stairs."

"Just means you get there first," Starkey replied. "And that's worth a little sweat."

"Yeah." Bug punched the up button on the elevator door. "But don't worry, I'll wait on you. Wouldn't want to steal your thunder."

Bug heard Starkey reply, "No jealously here," just as he opened the door and started running up the steps.

The elevator came to a smooth stop much too quickly for Bug's liking, but he exited with pistol drawn just in case. He hoped there weren't any cameras or that anyone would accidentally come out of their apartment while he made his way to 4G and then he quit hoping for anything as he focused all of his attention on staying alive.

Starkey opened the stairwell door and walked out with his pistol drawn. He had run up the steps two at a time so he was a bit out of breath, but he continued to run to Bug. They got to 4G about the same time, one took the left side, the other the right side.

Bug reached over and rapped on the door. There was no reply. Bug rapped once again. Still no reply. He then reached and twisted the door knob. He felt the door opening and he pushed it quickly and both he and Starkey lay back against their respective walls.

There was no sound from the apartment and there were no shots coming through the door. They waited about ten seconds and then Starkey made a motion to Bug with his hand indicting he was going in low. Bug nodded and then Starkey made his move, moving quicker than a fifty year old had a right to move. Starkey moved quicker than a twenty year old had a right to move.

Bug followed Starkey into the room, keeping as low as possible for a guy that was over six feet tall and more than forty pounds overweight. Bug would later tell that he had been faster than the Flash at getting into the room.

Once inside, they could see that the fireworks had already happened. Reinlein the well-built security chief had not been well built enough. He was lying on the apartment floor, surrounded by blood that wasn't likely to come out of the carpet easily. It appeared Wreek had lost his security deposit. He was sprawled out in the kitchen. He at least appeared to be alive. There was a silenced .45 calibre pistol very close to both bodies. Fireworks had been right.

"Call the cops or split?" Bug asked.

"Since Wreek is still alive we call the cops. Maybe it's time we brought them into our little deal anyway. See if you can stop the blood flowing. I'll check Reinlein, but it looks to me like he's shuffled off this mortal coil."

Bug nodded, then went into the adjoining bathroom and found a couple of towels. He had been taught basic first aid, as it was mandatory for all investigators at National, but he didn't remember any of it. He did seem to recall you applied pressure to the wound to prevent blood flow and he did that hoping he wasn't killing Wreek in the process.

Starkey checked the carotid artery on the neck of Reinlein and did not feel a pulse. If he was alive then it was a very weak life and would not last until the ambulance arrived, thus Starkey left him as he lay and called 911 asking for both an ambulance and the police.

Starkey walked over to Bug and said, "Anything we need to get straight before the boys in blue arrive?"

"Call Gonzo," Bug said. "You'll make him a dear friend after hauling him out of bed two nights in a row."

Starkey growled, "Why don't you call him. I'll handle your guy while you do."

"Your lead on this," Bug replied. "Besides, Gonzo might not come down just because he hates me."

Starkey gave Bug a descriptor that wasn't quite a compliment then he hit his speed dial for Gonzo.

Bug was right, Gonzo wasn't a bit happy about being woken for the second time in as many days. "Starkey," Gonzo said. "You could clear up the overpopulation on this fair planet in no time at all if we could just assign you to enough cases."

"You gonna crack wise or you gonna come down here. The cops will be here any minute."

"I'm gonna do both," Gonzo said. "You and Bug know to keep quiet, let me do the talking and I'll let you know what to say and when to say it. I'm on my way."

Starkey hung the phone up and Bug said, "Any wisdom from Gonzo?"

"Yeah," Starkey said. "He advised me to go to a very warm place that ain't Florida."

Bug laughed. "Good ole Gonzo. I suppose he said don't talk until he gets here. Like we would do otherwise."

"You got it. So we don't talk when the cops get here but we can talk until they arrive. How you read this?"

Bug said, "Guys don't go shooting each other for no reason usually and pros like these guys never. Other than that, I don't know. It may be the $4 million or it may be one got too friendly with the other's girl. I suppose we'll find out eventually."

"Well," Starkey said. "That gold Caddy that Reinlein was driving looks like the car I saw parked at Bigg's place. That means this is definitely about the robbery in my book. I think Reinlein here is cleaning up after the robbery. However, I don't think he has the $4 million and I'm sure the others don't have it. Otherwise none of this makes sense."

The mournful sound of an ambulance and the jarring sound of a police car drifted into the apartment. Bug and Starkey didn't look any too pleased at what they heard but then again, who is when they knew the cops were coming.

BUG, STARKEY AND GONZO ARE GUESTS OF THE POLICE

The cops arrived as they always do and so did the ambulance. There were two young paramedics with a dolly leading the parade and behind them came two young policemen. All the old folks had earned enough seniority to be home at nights plus the young guys hadn't gotten cynical yet and they usually preferred the higher pay and the higher risk of night time policing and ambulancing.

One of the paramedics rushed towards Wreek and the other went to work on Reinlein. "This one's gone," the young man said as he gazed down on the body of Reinlein. "But I'll see if I can work some magic."

The other paramedic took over from Bug and said, "At least you didn't kill him."

Bug didn't crack wise for once and just smiled back. Then he finally stood and groaned since he had been in an uncomfortable position for way too long for a fat guy pushing fifty.

Starkey didn't recognise the two policemen, which wasn't unusual as he didn't do much work these days that concerned the police. Most of his work was divorce work and that meant tailing old men or old women, taking pictures of said old men or old women meeting younger men or younger women, and passing that off to a divorce attorney. Old guys didn't shoot at him, even when he was discovered. He liked it that way. This real police work stuff was for the birds.

'I'm officer Tomas," one of the young cops said. "And that's officer Newton. We need to have a few words with you and your partner."

"We've got a lawyer coming," Starkey said. "We will talk with you after we talk with him."

Bug laughed. "Good ole Gonzo. I suppose he said don't talk until he gets here. Like we would do otherwise."

"You got it. So we don't talk when the cops get here but we can talk until they arrive. How you read this?"

Bug said, "Guys don't go shooting each other for no reason usually and pros like these guys never. Other than that, I don't know. It may be the $4 million or it may be one got too friendly with the other's girl. I suppose we'll find out eventually."

"Well," Starkey said. "That gold Caddy that Reinlein was driving looks like the car I saw parked at Bigg's place. That means this is definitely about the robbery in my book. I think Reinlein here is cleaning up after the robbery. However, I don't think he has the $4 million and I'm sure the others don't have it. Otherwise none of this makes sense."

The mournful sound of an ambulance and the jarring sound of a police car drifted into the apartment. Bug and Starkey didn't look any too pleased at what they heard but then again, who is when they knew the cops were coming.

BUG, STARKEY AND GONZO ARE GUESTS OF THE POLICE

The cops arrived as they always do and so did the ambulance. There were two young paramedics with a dolly leading the parade and behind them came two young policemen. All the old folks had earned enough seniority to be home at nights plus the young guys hadn't gotten cynical yet and they usually preferred the higher pay and the higher risk of night time policing and ambulancing.

One of the paramedics rushed towards Wreek and the other went to work on Reinlein. "This one's gone," the young man said as he gazed down on the body of Reinlein. "But I'll see if I can work some magic."

The other paramedic took over from Bug and said, "At least you didn't kill him."

Bug didn't crack wise for once and just smiled back. Then he finally stood and groaned since he had been in an uncomfortable position for way too long for a fat guy pushing fifty.

Starkey didn't recognise the two policemen, which wasn't unusual as he didn't do much work these days that concerned the police. Most of his work was divorce work and that meant tailing old men or old women, taking pictures of said old men or old women meeting younger men or younger women, and passing that off to a divorce attorney. Old guys didn't shoot at him, even when he was discovered. He liked it that way. This real police work stuff was for the birds.

'I'm officer Tomas," one of the young cops said. "And that's officer Newton. We need to have a few words with you and your partner."

"We've got a lawyer coming," Starkey said. "We will talk with you after we talk with him."

Bug laughed. "Good ole Gonzo. I suppose he said don't talk until he gets here. Like we would do otherwise."

"You got it. So we don't talk when the cops get here but we can talk until they arrive. How you read this?"

Bug said, "Guys don't go shooting each other for no reason usually and pros like these guys never. Other than that, I don't know. It may be the $4 million or it may be one got too friendly with the other's girl. I suppose we'll find out eventually."

"Well," Starkey said. "That gold Caddy that Reinlein was driving looks like the car I saw parked at Bigg's place. That means this is definitely about the robbery in my book. I think Reinlein here is cleaning up after the robbery. However, I don't think he has the $4 million and I'm sure the others don't have it. Otherwise none of this makes sense."

The mournful sound of an ambulance and the jarring sound of a police car drifted into the apartment. Bug and Starkey didn't look any too pleased at what they heard but then again, who is when they knew the cops were coming.

BUG, STARKEY AND GONZO ARE GUESTS OF THE POLICE

The cops arrived as they always do and so did the ambulance. There were two young paramedics with a dolly leading the parade and behind them came two young policemen. All the old folks had earned enough seniority to be home at nights plus the young guys hadn't gotten cynical yet and they usually preferred the higher pay and the higher risk of night time policing and ambulancing.

One of the paramedics rushed towards Wreek and the other went to work on Reinlein. "This one's gone," the young man said as he gazed down on the body of Reinlein. "But I'll see if I can work some magic."

The other paramedic took over from Bug and said, "At least you didn't kill him."

Bug didn't crack wise for once and just smiled back. Then he finally stood and groaned since he had been in an uncomfortable position for way too long for a fat guy pushing fifty.

Starkey didn't recognise the two policemen, which wasn't unusual as he didn't do much work these days that concerned the police. Most of his work was divorce work and that meant tailing old men or old women, taking pictures of said old men or old women meeting younger men or younger women, and passing that off to a divorce attorney. Old guys didn't shoot at him, even when he was discovered. He liked it that way. This real police work stuff was for the birds.

'I'm officer Tomas," one of the young cops said. "And that's officer Newton. We need to have a few words with you and your partner."

"We've got a lawyer coming," Starkey said. "We will talk with you after we talk with him."

The two ambulance men had loaded Wreek onto the dolly and attached various forms of life saving drip bags to Wreek. Reinlein had been covered with a white sheet and declared DOA. He was now the problem of the forensics team and the medical examiner. Just as the ambulance team left the forensic team arrived. They shooed out the cops and Bug and Starkey after asking the basic question, "You guys touch anything?" and getting the reply of no from the cops and Bug and Starkey saying kinda since they were trying to save the lives of the shootees.

As the four awaited the arrival of Gonzo in the lobby Tomas continued to blast questions at both Bug and Starkey and received only polite smiles in response.

"I'll book you guys as material witnesses, so help me, so if you want to stay out of the drunk tank for the night you'd better open up."

Bug, who was a bit ashen faced since he wasn't all that used to seeing dead bodies and shot victims and the blood that goes with it said, "This ain't our first rodeo, officer. Go ahead and book us. I ain't gonna see anything worse in the drunk tank than I've seen tonight."

Officer Newton wanted to lower the temperature a bit. "Then you ain't seen our drunks."

Even Tomas laughed at that and it had the desired effect as there were no more questions and they all just stood there silently throwing mind darts at each other until Gonzo arrived.

Gonzo came in about five minutes later and said, "Starkey, don't expect a Christmas gift this year." Then he turned to the officers and said, "I need a few minutes with my fellow employees before they can talk with you. I suggest we go to your HQ where we can sit in one of your offices, but it's up to you. We can go back to our own homes and I will guarantee that

Starkey and Bug will give a statement to whomever needs to see them at any stated time tomorrow."

Tomas was about to reply when the elevator door opened and he was demoted to the second team. It was a detective of homicide, looking somewhat dishevelled. Gonzo knew it was Matthews and wasn't overly thrilled at the knowing.

"Thanks for holding them for me officers," Matthews said but there wasn't a lot of thanks in his voice, but there was dismissal. The two officers nodded and went back over to the apartment. The ME would finally tell them when they were no longer needed and then they had the report to complete. Some nights were just lousy.

"You National lads are finding way too many dead bodies," Matthews said. "I heard you found one last night too. You might want to fill me in."

Gonzo just smiled that knowing smile of his and said, "As I was telling the officers, I have not yet had time to talk with my fellow employees. I insist on that right and we can do it tomorrow or tonight, but I must have that opportunity."

Matthews just nodded and replied, "Don't like private cops a whole lot, and I like the lawyer of private cops even less."

Bug said in a quiet voice but loud enough for Matthews to hear, "Don't know how I'm gonna sleep tonight after hearing that."

Gonzo glared at Bug even though he knew it was useless.

Matthews, who really didn't like private cops or their lawyer said, "You got it then. Let's go back to HQ. I'm thinking you guys might be material witnesses or something else I'll think of on the way there. Have fun tonight with the drunks."

Starkey said to Bug, "Damn it, Bug."

Bug just shrugged.

"Newton," Matthews said. "Would you please take these two," Matthews pointed at Bug and Starkey, "down to the station and book them as material witnesses."

Newton jumped at the chance since it got him out of standing around doing nothing while the forensics boys did their thing. "You want me to cuff them?" Newton asked.

"Nah," Matthews replied. "But we will take your pistols, just in case."

Bug and Starkey gave the pistols to Matthews and he placed them in evidence bags and handed the bags to Newton. "Have fun, boys," Matthews said.

Gonzo said, "See you tomorrow boys, and for what it's worth, I think Matthews is a jackass too."

Matthews looked quickly at Gonzo, but saw that both Tomas and Newton were looking at him, so he just smiled and said, "Everybody gets to run their mouth in this free country of ours."

Gonzo felt he had pressed his luck enough and so he just smiled and then walked down with the trio as they headed to Newton's vehicle. "They'll keep you in lock up through the night, but I'll talk to cooler heads than Matthews and have this sorted out by ten at the latest. As I said, keep quiet, and if it's any consolation, it'll take them a couple of hours to book you, so most of the drunks will be asleep by the time they put you in the cooler."

Starkey didn't think that was any consolation at all but he nodded and so did Bug. Gonzo was a jerk sometimes, but he was their jerk and they appreciated what it meant when he irritated a cop in their defence.

Newton walked slowly behind the pair as they exited the building and showed them the way to his police car. Lots of people in the apartment building had been awakened by the noise and they were standing in their doorways watching the excitement.

They all looked closely at Bug and Starkey as they walked by. Bug even waved at a couple of them and would have waved at more except Starkey said, "Stop being a jerk, Bug."

They arrived at the police car and Bug said, "Shotgun."

Newton said, "You'll find the view much more to your liking in the back seat."

Newton opened the door and Bug and Starkey got in. Starkey said, "You know, Bug, you have the amazing talent of making any situation worse. It must win you many friends among your co-workers."

Bug just shifted his eyebrows and said, "I don't know that I got your personality, Starkey. I don't like being bullied and I don't like being disrespected, unless there is something the other guy can get out of the bullying or the disrespect. Matthews was just being crass. He did it because he could do it and knew there was nothing we could do back. So, I did something back. I'm sorry you have to pay for my sins, but I ain't sorry I sinned."

Starkey had nothing to say to that because he could see why Bug mouthed off and he himself wanted to mouth off. But he didn't know how Bug had made it this long in the private cop business. If you couldn't take crap from cops you typically don't have much of a career in the private investigation world.

Newton cranked the car and the radio came on. Newton was an oldies fan, and a rockabilly fan, so there were some songs by Bill Haley, and by Buddy Holly and others of that ilk. There was one by someone that Starkey couldn't place, and it was a song that definitely should not be sung as rockabilly. It was "Danny Boy". Bug heard the first few lines and said to Starkey, "Hear that? You know just cause something can be done, doesn't mean it should be done."

Starkey didn't smile, he just lay his head against the car and prayed for daylight.

OMEGA—THE MYSTERY COMES TO A SATISFYING (?) CONCLUSION

Never trust a man who says he is honest. He ain't. Never trust a guy who says he is dishonest. He is. Above everything, never trust yourself—you are lying to yourself much more often than you are telling the truth. Trust me on this.
—The wisdom (or lack thereof) of Bug

WHAT'S IN A NAME?

I got in the office bright and early and noticed that Bug wasn't at his desk drinking the sludge that passed for coffee in our office. That was unusual as Bug generally came in before me most mornings. I didn't think anything about it until I happened to see Thompson and he waved me into his office.

"Bug and Starkey were picked up by the cops yesterday," Thompson said. "After a homicide and as material witnesses. Gonzo is down at the station setting things right. I understand that there's a cross in your cases."

"Seems to be," I said. "The Cready case seems related to the Garson case and we think it's tied to the robbery at First National. If Bug and me recover the money, we aim to try for the reward."

"Shouldn't be a problem as your primary case and it's arguable that not even Starkey's primary case has anything to do with the robbery on the face of it. I'll back you, but corporate does what it does. So I wouldn't spend any of that money ahead of time. Give me the five minute version."

I started my nickel version. "There was something loopy about the accident that Cready was involved in, at least according to Cready. He said the body of the man supposedly killed in the accident was already cold. That meant the guy was dead and somebody lured Cready to the location so that an accident could be staged. Due to lot of unusual circumstances, the forensics guys couldn't affirm that, so Cready is on the hook for at minimum a car accident that might become vehicular homicide."

I took another deep breath and continued, "Starkey was hired by United Transhipment to trace a guy called Chuck Garson. Starkey found out that Garson had an alias, several as a matter of fact, but one was called

Leonard Rydell. Starkey was able to trace a phone call Garson had made to a bar called Smittee's. At Smittee's Starkey found that Garson was known as this Rydell. However, Starkey got the feeling that those he talked to at the bar were either lying or covering for Garson. Starkey identified some of the names of the other patrons of the bar, and among them were Tom Wreek, a driver for hire at anything crooked, and a strongman named Bigg Jones."

"Wreek was shot to pieces last night," Thompson said. "The guy that was shooting him was himself shot. A Jake Reinlein."

"I'll get to that connection in a moment," I said. "Since Starkey had found two guys that were possible bank robbers and since Butree—the guy that Cready hit—was a known electronic expert that had been involved with bank robberies in the past, we reasoned the two cases were related. And once I heard that Garson worked at a firm that might just accidentally on purpose launder money, I was much more certain that our cases dovetailed.

"Since it was likely that the Cready accident was set up, it was possible that Butree was dead and this was a roundabout way to get rid of the body so that the police wouldn't be suspicious, or at least not as suspicious at once, which might have been sufficient for our robbers to do what had to be done and then get out of town. From that I figured the guy had really been killed in a car accident, just on the day before. Therefore his death would look like a car accident, for the simple reason it was a car accident.

"Here's where we get to Jake Reinlein. Bug and me had our data guys track down all accidents on the morning of the fifteenth, the day of the robbery. There was a really bad one at an intersection where the Night of Colours dance club is located. The accident killed a drunk driver of a BMW who was at fault as he ran a red light, but the SUV that survived the crash ran. Since the club had a camera that looked like it might give us some info, I went over there to see what I could get. The chief of security was this Jake Reinlein and he gave me the footage I asked for, but he told me it had already been given to the cops, so he wasn't doing me any great favour."

I paused a moment and said, "Starkey had tailed one of the suspects, Bigg, to the Night of Colours, then he trailed Bigg home. Bigg was killed by person or persons unknown. I went to Smittee's last night to see what I could see and I saw it was a numbers joint and thus a shady place where shady deals are made. Bug was at the Night of Colours just to see what he could see last night, and Starkey was trailing Wreek. That's about it. If I could come up with a logical reason for the staged accident, I'd be a lot more certain of the wherefores and whatnots. But I have to say, it looks like a lot of chicanery for very little gain."

"What's your next move?" Thompson asked.

"I'm gonna go see skip trace. They were working Garson and trying to find out who owned Smittee's. I'll bet it's either the mob or United Transhipments, who seem to be working fairly closely with the mob boys. Then I was gonna see Starkey and Bug. I think it's time one of us made a house call on Mr Himley, who is supposed to just be a locksmith, but he appears to be involved in the robbery somehow. Since I think that two of his partners are dead and one is pretty shot up, he might be willing to spill a few beans."

Thompson nodded. "Gonzo has been working with some of our financial consultants and it seems it's an open secret that United Transhipments is a fancy name for money laundering are us. They likely called in Starkey to trace this guy Garson because he outsharped them and stole some of their stolen money. Corporate has already terminated the contract with United

Transhipments and given them their money back. Gonzo is going to tell the cops what we have learned thus far and then we are out of the finding Garson business, though I hated to see it go as they paid well."

"Does that mean you don't want me to see Himley?" I asked.

"Not at all. Since you are still pursuing the Cready case and he is a possible connection to that, go right ahead. If we uncover the missing funds in the process, then we do so. Even if you and Bug get the $100,000, I'm sure corporate will figure out how to make a buck or two out of it, and if nothing else it's great publicity."

I nodded. What that meant of course was that the search for Garson was ongoing, we just weren't gonna tell United Transhipment squat about what we found.

I walked over to skip trace to find out if there was anything new about either of the cases. Johnathan was his ever-friendly self and said as I walked up, "Roach, I'm running on caffeine here so I ain't exactly the best company."

"You ain't ever exactly the best company," I said and there was enough truth in the statement to make both of us laugh. "What's new on the Garson Creasy case?"

"A lot. First we found that Dublet Holdings owns both Smittee's and Night of Colours. Surprised?"

"Not particularly," I said. "I would have been a couple of days ago, at least by the revelation of their ownership of the night club. But since I heard about Reinlein's death, and the circumstances surrounding it, I can't really say I was surprised."

"Well, here's something that might make even you, the best detective in the whole wide world, sit up and take notice. I was able to trace one of the fake IDs that Starkey found inside Garson's apartment to a local university. Meet Gerald Petrovsky, a proud alumnus of

Dupree University, BS in Commerce and Business. Also, if I'm not wrong, and you know, I typically ain't, the birth name of Chuck Garson." Jonathan pushed the folder over to me. Inside was a photo that looked like it had been taken for a yearbook, and it showed someone that looked like Garson.

"How sure are you of this?" I asked.

"Very, but that's based on a facial recognition package that I ran the photos from United Transhipment through. I also ran this photo that I pulled from the internet, it was taken from the Dupree Tigers Yearbook from ten years ago. The package gives a 99.8% probability that the two photos are the same person. I know that some people look similar, but I'd be willing to state in a court of law that the probability of two people looking this similar is impossible unless they are the same person."

"Looks like I've got some more investigating to do," I said. "Can you get me a list of the graduates from Dupree the year that Petrovsky graduated?"

"It's in the folder. Along with the current addresses and phone numbers of those I could find that still reside in our fair city. That's the reason I'm running on caffeine, I was up all night putting these pieces together."

"And National Detective Agency appreciates it, Johnathan. And so do I, even if I don't give you anything but grief."

"Grief and a paycheck are about all I ask of this world," Johnathan replied. "Since I'm a realist."

I walked by Thompson's office and tossed the report to him. "Pass on to Bug and Starkey when they come in, or maybe it's if they come in, and I'll start calling this list of people as soon as I'm through with Himley."

"Okay," Thompson said. "I'd offer someone to help, but with the loss of United Transhipment as a client we don't have anyone except Cready's law firm to stick the expenses against. Do what you can, within reason, and I'll take the responsibility of the charges. Feinstein and whatits may squawk a little, but I don't think they will squawk enough to cause us trouble."

"Thanks," I said and headed towards the door. I was going to the locksmith to try to find the key to this puzzle.

THE LOCKSMITH, WILL HE UNLOCK?

Himley's locksmith shop had seen better days, and the guy sitting on the stool in that locksmith shop had seen better years. He was an old guy, even by my standards, and I was pushing fifty, and had grey hair that was turning white, and the whitening wasn't an improvement. The gravelled face was also turning white and looked like it was approaching what one sees on an albino. He looked more asleep than awake. When I walked in and his eyes fluttered open, he seemed more dead than alive.

"Afternoon, sir," he said in a voice that sounded like it had sucked in one too many Marlboro in its day. "How can I help you?"

"I need to talk to Mr Bart Himley," I said. "I understand he owns and works in this place."

"He owns it right enough," the old man said. "And he claims to work here." Then he laughed. "But I go days on end and don't see him. I can get his name and number for you if you need it."

"That's okay," I said. "I already have them."

As I walked out of the store, the old man took up his sleeping again. That place did about as much business as a bus stop in the middle of the Pacific Ocean.

I drove over to the address I had for Himley and it was in a very ritzy part of our fair city. A suburb I think is what they call it. While not a real mansion, it appeared to be a McMansion with large white columns, three storeys, and more living space in the foyer than I have in my whole apartment. The locksmith business, even though no one ever came to the store, appeared to be booming.

There is always the chance when you do a cold call—that is, coming to see someone without an appointment—that it will be a wasted trip. There is also always the chance that if you do call they will simply hang up and tell you to go ride a horse, in not so many words. I've used both methods in my career many times and I honestly can't say which is better, because they both work sometimes and they both don't work sometimes. The cold call worked this time.

I parked in the horseshoe driveway and walked up to the door. I rang the bell and it was opened almost immediately by Himley. "You a cop?" he said.

"Kinda," I replied. "I'm a private cop. David Roche, National Detective Agency. I guess you heard about Tom Wreek last night." I saw his eyes narrow ever so slightly at the mention of Wreek. "And I've a hunch that if I know of your connection to Wreek, the cops will also know. So, I imagine they'll be here before long. But maybe they don't know about you and Wreek, and maybe I won't tell them what I know, if you talk to me."

Himley smiled, but it was one of those, "I don't like you but I gotta put up with you" smiles. He stepped back from the door and said, "I ain't sure exactly what you're talking about. Tom Wreek and I are just drinking buddies. I do know that he got shot last night as I read the papers like the next guy, and I don't mind telling you anything you need to hear, if it will help Tom."

In a pig's eye, I thought, but I just returned his fake smile with a matching fake smile. I followed him into his fancy house and wondered who came up with the slogan that crime doesn't pay.

"I'd offer you coffee," Himley said, "but I don't want to encourage you to stay any longer than necessary."

At least he was honest and he deserved honesty in return. As soon as I settled into a comfortable chair, I faced him and said, "I think you and Tom Wreek were part of a gang that robbed the First National Bank in the early morning hours of the fifteenth. I also think that you were involved in a wreck that killed Randolph Butree—another member of your gang—as you were fleeing the robbery. I also know that Bigg Jones was your strong-armed guy and he has been killed. How am I doing so far?"

Himley looked at me with the same fixed smile and said, "Continue, I don't know what you are talking about but it is fascinating listening to that melodious voice of yours."

"Uh huh. Well, there are now two members of the gang dead and one shot. You're the last man standing, so to speak, and I figure you might need our help continuing to stand."

"That means what exactly?" Himley asked.

"That means, if you return the money, through us, the firm will give you legal counsel and we may also try to shield your identity from the police." I looked at Himley gravely. "The cops may not have as good a deal for you."

"The cops will do what is best for them and you don't know squat if you think I'm gonna own up to a bank job. But I will tell you this much. As I understand it, there was upwards of $4 million taken in that robbery. Do you think that if I had four mill I'd still be in this lousy burg? Just a hypothetical, you understand."

"I think that someone else has the money," I said. "That someone else is named Chuck Garson and you claim you know him as Leonard Rydell. At least that's how this seems to be playing out. Just an educated guess, but what do you think?"

"I don't think at all on the subject," Himley said. "Rydell was just a guy I drank with, just like Bigg and Wreek. If you had more than that, the cops would be here with you. Any other fairytales you wish to discuss before you leave my house and go and bother some other poor innocent?"

"Just a word of warning," I said. "United Transhipment owns Dublet Holding. Dublet Holding owns Smittee's and the night club, Night of Colours. They also own the land that Bigg lived on. Do they own this house?"

"Not yet," Himley replied. "Though I'd be willing to sell to them if the price was right. But you need to explain to me why I should care that United whatever owns anything. As far as I can recall, I never heard of them before."

"It means more to you than to me," I said. "These guys seem to play hardball. I know that Jake Rothlein was shot up plenty by Tom Wreek while he was returning the favour. I suspect that Rothlein killed Bigg Jones. I also suspect that United Transhipment has plenty of other Jake Rothleins on their payroll and they will pay you a visit, sooner rather than later. Maybe they want Garson, maybe they want the $4 million, but my guess is they want them both, and they ain't overly concerned about breaking eggs while they obtain both."

"Well, Mr Roche," Himley said, "I thank you for coming by today and telling me everything that you say I already know, but I don't think I am up to confessing to something I didn't do. Also, I will be more circumspect with my drinking partners in the days ahead. But your concern is appreciated."

"Just one more thing," I said. "I figure Garson is your go-to guy at United and that he was the guy that set up the money laundering for you. It seems United is looking for him for other reasons than just the four mill, though that is plenty reason enough. It is possible that Garson set up a deal with a fellow crook at the Swiss bank, and it is possible that Garson has not only the four mill, but lots of other money that you rightfully stole."

That was just a shot in the dark, but it seemed to make sense. After all, the story that Nebo told Starkey was pure moonshine. There was a lot of protection on laundered money, and just giving your password to your point of contact would not allow them to transfer any great amount of money from your account. The banks would want to confirm the withdrawals, because they might be on the hook if the money was fraudulently taken. But even if it was a shot in the dark, it seemed to hit ole Himley right between the eyes. He may have not only just lost his share of the four mill, but also his ill-gotten fortune.

"That would certainly be unfortunate for any of those that had money with these crooked banks," Himley said. "But then, it would likely be ill-gotten gains, wouldn't it, so maybe it's karma. But I suggest you take your information to some federal agency that tracks and cares about such things, as I do not have a horse in this particular race."

"Your loss," I said. "So think it over. If you go state's evidence on this, the boys in blue can get you into witness protection. It ain't this place," I waved my hand about the room indicating just how luxurious it was, "but it ain't a hovel and it sure ain't six feet under."

"Excellent advice," Himley replied with eyes that said he wanted to get on to other things, and I imagined that those things included calling someone at the Swiss bank and checking on his account. "If I meet a man who's part of this robbery and has money in some crooked bank I'll pass it on to him. Now you really must excuse me, as I have a busy day ahead of me."

I stood and let myself be escorted from the room. I walked to my car and looked back over my shoulder but Himley wasn't watching me; I imagine he was already on the phone trying to find out if his funds were safe. If there was any justice in the world, the funds would be long gone, but there is seldom any justice in the world.

I drove back to headquarters. I also picked up a tail. It seems United Transhipment did not appreciate having their contract cancelled.

THE OLD COLLEGE TRY

I got back to HQ about 2 p.m. and my tail had left me two blocks earlier. They figured I was going to National, I assumed. Either that or they just wanted me to report I was trailed, which I did right away.

Bug and Starkey were in the meeting room getting updated by Johnathan and Thompson, and I walked in and gave them the hi sign. Bug waved back, Starkey seemed to be in lesser spirits however as he just nodded.

I sat down at the table and began to drink that noxious brew the office claimed was coffee and listened to the tail end of a repeat of what I was told earlier today. After Johnathan finished I spoke up, saying, "Just for the record, Mr Bart Himley ain't never heard of nothing about no robbery and the fact that all of his drinking buddies are getting popped is bewildering to him, but there is no connection to him. Also, I picked up a tail while at Himley's. I figure it's United Transhipment."

Starkey said, "While trail you and not me?"

"Don't really know but I think they had Himley's place staked out and followed me because they saw me leave Himley's. If they ran the plates on the car, and they would because we would, they'd find that it was a company car and thus know I worked for National. I believe they'll follow either of us since they really want to know where their boy Garson is, for a lot of reasons."

Starkey nodded and Bug asked of Thompson, "Do we shake them or not, boss?"

"By all means shake them," Thompson said. "If for no other reason than professional pride. We can't let ourselves be followed about if we know about it, unless we have a reason for it, like leading someone into a trap."

"Got it," Bug said.

"Good," Thompson said. He then passed each of us a folder. "Johnathan has taken the names of all of those that graduated with Garson/Rydell/Petrovsky from Dupree and who still live in this city, and broken their addresses into three contiguous sections. Each of you will have the names in one section; there are about forty names on each list. Call them first but see if you can find out anything about Petrovsky that might lead us to his alter ego of Garson. If you do go and see anyone of these people, shake and if necessary rattle and roll your tail. The last thing we want to do is to provide United Transhipment with any new information."

Starkey, Bug and I all nodded. Johnathan and Thompson left the meeting room so we could talk among ourselves. I could tell that Bug and Starkey weren't exactly happy and what's more weren't happy at all with each other. They looked tired and sleepy and agitated all at once, and that meant they weren't gonna be worth a damn at cold calling, since you needed to be polite at a minimum. They looked grumpy enough to snap the head off a preacher for just saying good morning.

"You guys go home and get some sleep," I said. "I'll get through as many of these names as I can on the list and we'll meet back in the morning and divvy up the remainder."

"Who died and made you boss?" Bug asked. "It sure wasn't Thompson as I just saw him walk out the door."

"Have it your way then," I said. "Just trying to be nice."

"That'll be the day," Starkey said and laughed. Bug laughed too. It was almost a case of the giggles. I just shrugged. I'd been in the drunk tank, and then been interrogated by the cops a few times myself. You might get something from the experience, like head lice from one of the drunks, but you don't get any sleep from it.

Since my attempt at kindness was rebuffed, I just grabbed up my list and left Bug and Starkey to their lists, then I headed back to my desk for one of the worst parts of being an investigator. Cold calling.

Trying to get someone to talk to you on the telephone in this day and age is a nightmare. Our society is so inundated with robocalls, that they typically don't answer the phone at all, just let the answering machine screen the calls. Once you've left the message that you're a private cop wanting to get information for your own purposes and nothing for their gain, they typically just delete the message. Still we cold called, because someone in our organisation had done a study showing it's more effective than just going to the houses of those who may or may not have the information you desire. Sometimes the cold call does work and when it does, even if only one out of ten times, that has saved a lot of shoe leather and a lot of investigator time. The corporate office likes that.

I had gotten through about twenty-five or twenty-six calls when I finally got a hit. A gal named Mrs Mildred Johnson picked up her phone and when I told her I was trying to trace one Mr Gerald Petrovsky she said, "What's Gerry got into this time?"

"I take it you know him then?" I asked. "We're interested in his background, he has applied for a Government position and we're just doing a security check. So, anything you can tell us about him would be of help."

"Well," Mrs Johnson replied hesitantly, "I didn't know him except through Mavis. She dated him and I thought they would marry, but they didn't. Gerry was just another guy to me."

"Can you give me the full name of Mavis? Phone number and address would be nice also."

"Her name was Mavis Bautner in college and we were great friends there. I've not seen her since, even though I think she still lives in the city. She married, and I think she divorced, but this is just what I saw on Facebook. I really don't know how to contact her. Sorry."

"Don't be," I said. "You've helped immensely."

I wrote up our conversation in the phone log. I might go and see her or I might not. If she was telling the truth I wouldn't need to.

I walked over to see Johnathan. He was reading Drudge as he often does.

"Hate to interrupt your busy day," I said, "but we have things afoot here."

"You know," Johnathan said, "if I ever meet a detective that doesn't have things afoot then I think I'll buy him a drink and shake his hand. What you need, oh mighty one?"

"There's a possible connection to Garson/Petrovsky, a lady named Mavis Bautner. She dated Garson when he was known as Petrovsky and they were at Dupree together. Can you dig up a photo of this lady and also see if you can get her current address. I need to go and sorta discuss things with her."

"Gimme fifteen minutes," Johnathan said. "Have a cup of coffee. I'm buying." He pointed at the office coffee stand.

"You the man," I said, and went back to my desk, giving the coffee stand a wide berth. I continued to make cold calls, and continued to get answering machines until Johnathan came back to see me.

"Mavis Bautner matriculated from Dupree the same year as Mr Petrovsky. Her dad, Lester Bautner, is quite wealthy, owning several different businesses of various and sundry kinds. She married a Phil Campain a few years back, but it didn't take. She currently resides with daddy dearest at a house in a quite upscale part of town, being evidently what is known as a boomerang, them that divorce and go home to mommy and daddy. She's working as an executive vice president at a place called Ramparts. They're some sort of online news agency, and yes the place is owned by her father. Better to be born lucky than good type thing. If there's a connection between her and Petrovsky, it didn't leap out and grab me."

I noted the address and saw it was one of the gated communities that are very difficult to surveil. I knew I wouldn't just be driving up to her door and knocking. You gotta have a legitimate reason to get into a gated community and I do mean legitimate. The guards wouldn't let the President into the community without first checking in triplicate with the people that he was supposed to be seeing.

Johnathan had provided me with several pictures of the lady. She was average looking, nothing unremarkable or remarkable about her, just another person that just happened to be born rich.

I went over to Thompson's office and told him what Johnathan had come up with and I also wanted authorisation to trail the lady without first talking to her.

"You have no indication that she will lead you to Garson/Petrovsky," Thompson said. "I'd think you would want to talk with her first, and then decide if a tail is warranted."

"Here's my thinking," I said. "And why I want to tail her with no prior contact."

Thompson nodded at me to continue.

"If I was a desperate man, and I think Garson is desperate as it appears that he's being hunted for by lots of people and some of those people seem to want him dead, then I would want a hidey hole that was not easily traced. Since this lady may have once been at least a hot item in his history, and since she ain't gotten any prettier since college and is divorced, I might just conveniently remember that and give her a call. I wouldn't tell her that I was a money launderer or that I had just stole $4 million, but I'm sure I could concoct some story that would satisfy her. She would then, quite reasonably given the fact her dad has quite a few bucks, give me shelter and not even think twice about it just so she could see if the old flame could be reignited."

"That makes sense," Thompson said. "But why not just go see her at her workplace, explain the situation and see if she'll divulge the location, if she is indeed hiding him. You can always put a tail on her to see if she rabbits to him."

"Oh, she might be inexperienced enough to rabbit to him, but I do think he would have warned her not to come see him if anyone, cop or not, came to talk with her about him. I think she may want to go and see him on her own, and probably has several times since he came back into her life. Either that or she isn't hiding him. I think the only way to be sure is to tail her for a few days, without bracing her first. But it's your decision."

Thompson thought for a moment. "There is no way I can make this a paying proposition." He just shrugged his shoulders. "All right, two days, three at the tops. If Bug or Starkey come up with a better lead I may pull you off. If they don't come up with something better, I'll shoo them over to help with the surveillance. Until I do, you will have to handle it yourself."

"Can do," I replied. Then I headed back to my desk and picked up the file. Ms Bautner was about to have company for a few days.

GONZO THE EXPLAINER

Gonzo had always known he was in the wrong profession, but after spending four years in prelaw, three years in law school, and then a year earning squat as an intern, you can't just say, "I hate this life" and move into something else. At least you can't if you want to earn a living and keep the wife from giving you the heave-ho.

There were good parts and bad parts about being a lawyer, just as there is with any profession. The trouble was, the bad parts outweighed the good parts significantly, at least in Gonzo's way of thinking. But you gotta do what you gotta do, and so he was a lawyer for a bunch of private cops who delighted in bedevilling him.

In order to obtain the release of Bug and Starkey, Gonzo had allowed them to sign a statement that told essentially the truth. They were on different cases but both seemed to merge as one and thus they were each trailing one of the shooters. Gonzo would not allow them to give the names of the customers they were trailing those men for. But he made the commitment that he would, once he consulted with his own bosses, come back and give them all the details and that those details might be of use to the police in an ongoing case.

The cops hadn't liked it, but on the other hand, they knew that Gonzo might go to the DA and create havoc if they didn't release the two investigators. Since they had nothing on them, except that Matthews didn't like them, they were going to have to release them soon anyway.

So Gonzo had gotten his approvals and he was back to discuss things with the Robbery division head. And he hated it. But then Gonzo hated most things, including himself most days.

After he'd given all the info to a Captain Harris—a balding, fat, cigar chomping cop who looked like a cop should look, unkempt—Harris nodded and said, "Yeah, we think that the foursome you mentioned—Butree, Wreek, Bigg and Himley—are good for the First National job. We didn't know about this United Transhipment involvement however, so I'll reach out and touch the feds on that one. They're the ones to deal with money laundering for the most part. You really think the accident was a set up?"

"Don't know," Gonzo said. "But it was how we got involved in this mess to start with and it's beginning to look more and more like it was a set up. We still don't have a reason why. For instance, why go to all the trouble to make it look like an accident? Just dump the body any old where and go own with your business."

"I believe we've found your reason for you," Captain Harris said. "It seems at 5 a.m. on the fifteenth Butree was involved in a marathon poker session with Wreek, Himley and Bigg. There's a DVD that proves it, since the bar Smittee's has a video camera that documents the session. It would prove inconvenient for the body to be found, or for Butree to be missing, given that alibi. So, the guys decided to find a logical reason for why Butree was dead."

Gonzo smiled. "That would make sense. You know what else would make sense, if some enterprising policeman would serve a warrant and look for traces of Mr Butree dead, not alive, in Smittee's. The gang had to hide the body somewhere and since Smittee's seems to be tied into the case, it might be interesting to see what a good forensics team would find."

"Given what you have just told me," Harris said, "I can likely pull one off. We'll shut down the numbers game if nothing else. It'll drift elsewhere, but it'll be good for a headline or two. The DA is thinking of running for mayor once the old cluck we have bites the dust, which may not take a whole lotta time since he's already older than dirt. Having a bust showing you're clamping down on the numbers racket wouldn't hurt. Liberals hate the numbers game cause the Government don't get a share of it, like the lottery. Conservatives hate the numbers game cause they think it only benefits the crooks. They're both right but the type of guy that plays the numbers game ain't one to do a whole lotta philosophising about it, he just thinks he might beat the odds. Few of 'em ever do, of course, but that don't stop 'em from trying."

"Do what you will with the numbers business," Gonzo said, "but National needs to know if you find something that will impact Mr Cready's case. We have standing in the matter since we are under contract with Feinstein and Gray. The information should be released to them also, since they are the law firm that is acting as legal counsel for Mr Cready."

"I think the DA will be happy to share," Harris said. "But you and his team work out those arrangements. If we do clear Cready, that's an even better story for the DA, he can tell how the valiant and ever diligent police has prevented a rush to judgment that would have condemned a man to prison. A miscarriage of justice averted by the ever faithful DA. I just wish Cready was a minority, that would be the topper."

"One can't have everything," Gonzo said.

"We can do some business with what you've given me. And we thank you for the honesty. Often, we're at odds with each other, so it's nice to be on the same team for once."

"As you say," Gonzo agreed.

"Now that we've gotten the stuff you are willing to share out of the way," Harris said, and he shifted the unlit cigar in his mouth, "we want the information you don't want to share. What do you know about the location of the $4 million taken in the robbery?"

"National is not under contract with First National and we have no interest in the matter," Gonzo said. "Except as good and law abiding citizens. If we knew the location of any stolen funds, we would of course provide that information to the police. It would be our civic duty."

"Yeah," Harris growled. "And the mayor might just believe in fiscal responsibility for the city, just like he always states. The reward money wouldn't have anything to do with your silence, would it?"

"Not a bit of it," Gonzo assured him.

"Uh huh. Well, just be advised that if we found out after the fact that you guys held back info that could have helped us recover the money, we'll be having a different sort of talk."

Gonzo nodded. "National has been in business for over a hundred years. We are always obliging when it comes to helping the police, but we aren't dopey enough to give you guys our best guesses on issues. Lawsuits happen that way."

"Lawsuits happen anyway," Harris said. "Just a word to the wise."

"If and when we uncover vital information," Gonzo said, "and when we are certain of our client privilege on a situation, then we will provide that information to the police. We will not provide information not required by law, ethics, or business judgment. That is how National has lasted as a business for over a hundred years. But you do what you think best at the time you think it. We have a lot of lawyers and, unlike me, some are very good at it."

"Okay," Harris said. "I don't want to end this on an unfriendly note, since we do appreciate the information. Since we now know that Smittee's is likely a mob front, and possibly the start of at least one money laundering scheme in this city, we will do our best to get a search warrant. Also knowing that Smittee's is owned by Dublet which is owned by United Transhipment gives us an excuse to raid that place. I'd like to do it sooner rather than later, because we'll bring the feds in on the money laundering. Once the feds are brought in they get touchy when we step on their turf and they may see Smittee's as their turf."

"And you'll inform us of anything you find that might be of use to our client Mr Cready?" Gonzo asked.

"I already told you that's the DA's decision," Harris said. "But we both know how discovery works, and the DA would be setting himself up for a lawsuit and even worse—bad publicity—if he withheld probative information from you. I wouldn't worry that pretty head of yours."

"Since my head is anything but pretty I have no fear of that. Captain Harris, it's been a pleasure, or at least as much of a pleasure as talking to a cop can be."

"And the same for me, Mr Gonzales," Harris replied. "Seldom do I talk to a mouthpiece and not have the urge to slam my fist down his throat. This discussion was one of the few. Maybe I'm mellowing in my old age."

"I doubt that," Gonzo said as he stood up. "I doubt that very seriously."

Gonzo walked out of the room leaving a smiling Captain Harris. That was a win, at least in the world of cops and lawyers.

THE TAIL

When you're on stake-out by yourself, you learn in a hurry that you can't drink a lot of coffee, cause it seems the world always works this way, the moment you go to the restroom is the same damned moment the person you're trying to tail takes off for parts unknown.

Since you can't drink coffee and you sorta kinda have to stay alert, you learn to sit quietly and slap your face every time the boredom hits. It must look odd to the casual passer-by as she sees what appears to be a rational man slapping himself, but then you don't much care what other people think of you or you wouldn't be a private cop to start with.

Another thing that will keep your mind engaged is to play the "who do I kick in the seat of the pants" game, where you remember all the sleights and all of the crap rendered unto you by others and think of just the right verbiage and rejoinders that would have put them in their place.

I was on about my third go round of both slaps and kick game when the prey, one Ms Mavis Bautner, came out of her place of employment and headed towards the parking area just down the street from her office building. I made sure the GPS was on so that I could get the exact location of wherever we wound up and tried to make myself more interested in the tail than I was. The truth is, while it may seem exciting to the uninitiated, tailing is mostly boring, from the wait to pick up the mark, to the here's where the mark is, it's mostly just sitting or driving and we all do more of that in our life than we care to.

The Bautner woman came out of the parking area and I pulled in about three cars back of her. I wasn't concerned that she would see me, cause she probably wouldn't—few people can spot a tail unless the guy doing the tailing is clumsy enough to fall right in behind the person. This only goes for a busy street, of course. If there are only two cars on the road, the odds of discovery goes up a whole lot for some reason.

Mavis Bautner was driving some exotic foreign car, not a Jag or a Porsche but something similar to one of those. I gotta admit unless I see the name plate I'm crap when it comes to identifying an automobile. She didn't seem to drive either too fast or too slow, nor was she meandering. Wherever she was going, she seemed to be going straight, at least right now, as we stayed on the same street for at least twenty blocks. Finally, she made a turn down towards the harbour district.

Since I was a couple of cars back and caught a red light, I couldn't tell exactly where she went down that street, but it gave me a new place to stake-out. If she was going to meet her old lover and coming from her office, then I could set up here and resume the chase tomorrow.

Just in case I got lucky, I went down the street she had taken and found it led right to the docks. There were a tonne of different type of ships and boats and restaurants and you name it. The harbour was always a place that had a lot of people and even more so in the daylight and around lunch, as people would come down to eat at one of those famed restaurants. I pulled into several of the restaurant parking lots, cruised slowly about looking for her bright red foreign job to no avail. If she was having lunch here, it didn't seem to be at some of the more famous places.

I took the main drag down the docks, the final road before land gave way to sea. There were several houseboats and yachts that were in their various slips all up and down the street. There were a lot of foreign red cars parked in some of those driveways but I didn't spot Mavis Bautner's. Finally, I gave it up and headed back to the intersection where she'd turned from the main street to the street that lead to the docks. I wanted to scout it out and see if there was a decent location to watch from.

I found a parking station and hauled my vehicle into it and followed the various ramps until I got to the top. From there I found I could see far down both streets and that was exactly what I wanted. If I could find another parking station at the end of the street that led to the dock, I could get Bug or Starkey to help. We might just be able to close in on exactly where Ms Bautner was going. I also had a thought that might save us the trouble of doing anything, because the city, God bless 'em, required all those beautiful slips to be registered and a tax paid on each and every one of them. And whatever the city taxed, they required a list of who had to pay those taxes, and that list would be somewhere in some database, and our dear Johnathan might just find that list for me.

I pulled out my spy glasses and stood at the top of the parking station looking down towards the dock, hoping to see Ms Mavis Bautner heading back towards her place of work. I also took out my phone and got Johnathan on the line.

"Hate to pull you away from your obvious important work of seeing naked women on the internet but I need a small favour," I said.

"Roach," Johnathan said. "A small favour to you would be to knock off the President. What you need besides a better tailor and a better job?"

"You mentioned this Bautner lady's father was quite wealthy," I said. "It occurred to me that he might have a houseboat or a yacht where someone could be stashed with reasonably little fear of discovery. Can you check the tax rolls and see if that guess pans out?"

"Gladly," Johnathan said. "I'll check both for him and his daughter, it's easy enough. Call you back in five."

"Thanks," I said and meant it. If I found a place to go to rather than having to just sit around on my brains all day, I would be a much happier private investigator.

As I waited for Johnathan's reply, I kept my eye glasses on the street leading from the docks. Sure enough, the red car was coming back towards the intersection. It was Mavis and she was alone. That made me a lot more certain that we were onto something. Whether that something wound up being our missing Mr Garson or just my wild imagination was yet to be discerned.

Just as the red car hit the intersection I could see it was an Alfa Romeo and that meant Ms Bautner had a lot more money than sense. Who'd pay seventy thousand for a car that was equivalent to many another car that cost forty. Well the rich are different I suppose.

Ms Bautner turned the corner and headed back towards her work. I didn't follow as I didn't care where she was going, I just wanted to know where she had been. The phone rang and I answered.

"Mr Lester Bautner owns Slips 144 C and 251 D," Johnathan said. "It seems his yacht is at 144 C and a houseboat is at 251 D. I don't know the difference between a yacht and a houseboat personally."

"About one hundred and fifty thousand," I replied. "From my less than encyclopaedic knowledge on the subject. Thanks. You can go back to the naked women now."

"What makes you think I wasn't seeing them all along? I have two screens for a reason."

I left my eagle's perch and headed back towards the dock. It was easy enough to find both of the slips and both had boats or ships or whatever you call those floating things that are big enough to float and for people to live on them at the same time. Having two to cover complicated the game and I didn't like complications but then few people do.

    I called it a day and headed back to the office to talk with Thompson. It was time to get the cops involved, since we may need warrants and such. Those would be easy to obtain if I perjured myself and said I'd seen Garson on one of them. I didn't know if I wanted to go that far, but I have to admit fifty thousand is a good enough reason to lie if you had to lie to see justice done anyway.

THE ALIBI

Captain Harris from Robbery was in Thompson's office when I came in. Thompson gave me the come hither sign and I came hither. They were watching TV.

"You know Captain Harris?" Thompson asked. "He's here to share some intel with us on the Cready and possibly the Garson case."

"Of course I know Captain Harris," I said. The jerk had arrested me at least twice in my career. The charges never stuck and he knew at the time they wouldn't, but he, like a lot of other cops, liked to discourage the private cop biz. Too much competition.

"Good to see you, Roche," Harris said and managed to maintain a straight face, which was acting deserving of an Oscar.

I sat down next to Thompson in a chair that he had just pulled up for me and watched the four men that we had been chasing for the past few days playing a fun game of poker. The time code ran at the bottom of the video and it showed the fifteenth of the past month and 4.32 a.m. They seemed to be having a lot of fun and they seemed to be fairly awake for four guys who'd been up all night.

"We got this from the guy that runs Smittee's," Harris said. "Bartender named Sacks. We've got him on illegal gambling since you guys were right about it being a numbers drop."

"Well," I said. "This means that either the data is manipulated or else Cready was mistaken about Butree already being dead at the wreck. My money is on the date being bogus."

"It likely is," Harris said. "Since the date comes from the recording device itself and anyone can set that to whatever they please, then it's not a very good alibi. But then if you're just trying to keep the Robbery cops off your backside for long enough to split the loot and then split yourself it might not have to be that good an alibi. It would, for instance, prevent us from jailing them for a while, just because there's a possibility that it's true. Also, Sacks swears he saw them there that night. We'll break that of course, since we got some serious charges headed his way, and before it's over, he'll be willing to swear the Pope's a Jew before we're through with him."

"There's other news," Thompson said. "Since the police searched Smittee's last night, they were able to send their forensic people in to see what evidence the nerds could find. They found something very useful for both us and the police. Did you know that Smittee's used to be a restaurant? They just changed over to a bar about five years ago, and they still have a freezer in the back of the bar. The forensic team found blood drops that they can tie to one Randolph Butree."

"That is good news," I said. "So it seems that Butree was killed in the accident and they stashed his body in the freezer until they could figure out a legit way to kill him. Cready seems to be off the hook."

"Likely so," said Harris. "We've also got the feds helping us with the laundering scheme. It seems United Transhipment likes making money so much they decided to expand into laundering not only drug money and numbers money, but any sort of stolen loot at all. The feds are ready to swoop any moment. They'd like to have Garson of course, but he's not all that important in the scheme of things."

"He may not be to you," I said, "but he is to me. He was evidently tied into this from the git go and he likely knows that Butree was dead on the fifteenth and can testify to that. While I don't doubt we can get Cready off with what we have now, it still would be better if we had concrete testimony that'd clear him."

"We want him as well," the Captain assured me. "There is still the matter of the missing $4 million. That has to still be in the wind, or else all of these killings make no sense."

"I agree," I said. "Have you guys had a chance to talk to Wreek? Is he even gonna recover?"

"Likely he will," Harris said. "And he may talk or he may not. You know crooks, some of them have a code and some don't; those that have a code and live by it will spend thirty years in stir just to spite the cops. They'll think they are doing it for their code of course, but it's really for their vanity."

"Himley?" I asked.

"Under surveillance but we haven't picked him up yet," Harris said. "I doubt he'll talk, and it's mostly because I think he was the guy that came up with the scheme to start with. Evidently he's been in the robbery business for quite a while and he's never been arrested or even suspected before. At least we think that, since he's moved from city to city over the past ten years and there's always a big robbery in the city he just left—just before he left. We probably won't get him on those, but if he starts to talk we might, so he won't talk. We should still be able to get him on this, however, and he's now part of our known crooks, so that will hinder him some in the future."

Harris changed the subject and asked Thompson, "You guys think you know where Garson is? We've run through all of our databases and talked to several known associates as they say, though the known associates we know about are fellow United Transhipment employees. Since they want him as badly as we do he likely didn't let them know anything that could trace him, assuming he was planning this for awhile."

"I think he's been planning this for a long while," Thompson said. "When Starkey first interviewed Nebo at United Transhipment, they said that Garson's accounts were being embezzled. There's likely some truth to that, though we now think United was just trying to trace Garson to get to the $4 million. If you assume Garson was a tad suspicious that his higher ups were onto his shenanigans, it makes sense that he'd plan on a big score to help him get away."

"It's obvious that the people that run United Transhipments are not the kind to be trifled with," Harris said. "Given that, Garson likely hid his trail as best he could prior to absconding with the funds."

"Where does this leave us?" I asked.

"We find Garson," Thompson said. "Or at least we locate him. We'll give the info to Captain Harris here and he'll be happy to go get him and bring him to justice. That okay with you, Captain?"

"Certainly," Harris said. "You give us the location and probable cause and we'll do the rest."

I kept quiet on what I knew, since I was certain that Thompson knew it too and would have likely spilled the beans if he thought Harris should know about the slips. There was still something amiss here, at least on the surface, or Thompson would have spoken.

"Thanks for bringing this by, Captain," Thompson said as he ejected the DVD and handed it back to Harris.

"Keep it," Harris replied and nodded at the DVD. "It may be useful in your case and we've already turned a copy over to Feinstein and Gray since they're representing Cready. I just wanted to go over the cases with National to see if we had anything new to go on and to let you know what we had found at Smittee's. You folks have been a pleasure to work with on both the Garson and the Cready case and I wanted to show the Department's appreciation."

"Always glad to help the police," Thompson lied and gave the biggest crocodile grin I had ever seen.

"No need to stretch the truth," Harris grinned back. "You'll let us know if you get a lead on Garson."

"My phone will be in my hand and your number will be hit as quickly as I can," Thompson said.

Harris waved and left. Thompson held up one finger at me to keep me from talking. He waited until he saw that Thompson had exited the building and then he said, "Meet me at room three, David, I've another case to discuss with you."

I nodded, since that meant he was afraid Harris had left a bug and since room three was on the other end of the building, it was the least likely place to be bugged.

I followed Thompson down to room three and was not overly surprised that there were three gents in black suits already sitting there.

"Meet Donovan, Jackson and Mulavey," Thompson said. "Special agents for the Federal Bureau of Investigation."

I shook hands with the three men. Each seemed to be a clone of the other: ramrod backs, lean almost to haggard, dark suit, narrow tie, average to good looks. They looked like they'd be the life of the party.

"We understand," said the agent I thought was Donovan, "that you may have discovered the location of Chuck Garson."

I looked at Thompson and he nodded that I should talk. I would rather Gonzo had been there, not because I trust him any more than I trust Thompson, but if you can blame your lawyer for a bad decision, things typically go better for you than blaming your boss.

"There are two slips owned by Lester Bautner," I said and I gave them the addresses and slip numbers. "I don't claim Garson is staying at one or the other, just that I have a suspicion that he's staying at one or the other."

I told the feds of the relationship that Johnathan had uncovered between Garson/Petrovsky and Mavis

Bautner. "It is tenuous," I admitted, "but it's all we've been able to uncover in the past few days of intense investigation. I think it's enough for you guys to get a warrant, but then I'm not a lawyer so my thoughts on the subject are not all that germane."

"Should be sufficient," Donovan said, and the other two agents nodded. I figured they were lawyers since most of the agents I had ever met—which weren't many for sure but still more than a few—had been lawyers.

"Thank you for your cooperation," Donovan said. "We'll take it from here." Which was cop speak for get lost.

I just smiled and nodded. I'd get the scoop on them from Thompson but we for sure weren't gonna just let them swoop in and grab our prey. The world doesn't work that way.

The three agents filed out of the room, heading to wherever FBI agents go to when they aren't out bothering real people. As quick as they left, Thompson said, "Let's go to my office and talk some."

I stopped on the way to Thompson's office, which was eighty-seven steps from meeting room three if it mattered, to grab some office coffee. I had a feeling I was going to need some strong stuff before the day was over.

Once we got into Thompson's office, he gave me the low down. "The feds think the locals are dirty," he said. "And they called corporate to have them talk with me. We are not to reveal anything about the location of Garson to the locals unless we must, so we don't volunteer anything. That's why the feds came over. They think and maybe rightly so, that United Transhipment must have some high and mighty officials in their back pocket in order to more or less launder their funds openly. I don't know that I agree, since most cops are trained to bust heads and confiscate drugs and that doesn't a financial analyst make. But regardless of my feelings on the matter, corporate has given me direction and we shall follow it."

"The local cops are small time corrupt," I said. "At least some of them. They'll take a fifty to give you something you're gonna get anyway just later. But I've never met one that would gladly let a big fish get away just for money. I'm sure it happens, but not as much as you'd expect."

"The feds think they're corrupt," Thompson said. "That's enough for our current situation. What that will mean in our long-term relationship with the locals, I don't know, but we follow orders like the next guy, and will worry about the fallout if and when it happens."

"So, we back off and let the feds come in?"

"We let the feds come in," Thompson replied. "And they can rouse Garson. But we still look for the $4 million. Besides, the feds can't keep us from parking where in the hell we want. And if we happen to decide to park where we can keep an eye on these two slips, then we might witness a raid or two, and who knows if anything'll come of that."

I nodded. "I'll take the yacht, there's a restaurant just across the street with easy parking. I'll go in and give the owner or manager a C note and make up a story. Who are you gonna put on the houseboat?"

"Starkey," Thompson said. "And I'll have Bug act as relief man for the two of you. He can set up wherever it's convenient to sub for you and Starkey. Between the three of you, work out whatever is required to make sure someone is there to observe both slips at all times. My bet is that it'll happen at two or three in the morning. It'll take the feds a while to get the warrant but I figure that'll happen by close of business today. So they hit the two slips at the same time and early in the morning when the subject of the search is likely to be half asleep and less likely to throw lead their way. Go home, grab a nap, and get there no later than 10 p.m."

"Got it," I said. "But I'd rather have another relief man than Bug. He and I haven't been getting along all that well of late, especially after our trip down south. How about Hanaran?"

"Fine," Thompson said, but his eyes narrowed. I was likely on shaky ground, but fifty thousand will make a man take chances.

I went by Johnathan's on my way out of the building and asked about the holdings of Lester Bautner. I heard the name of something that pleased me. Then I went home and tried to sleep but couldn't. I watched baseball instead. I also called Bug. He said okay and hoped we didn't get fired.

THE RAIDS

I just got through talking with Bug on the phone when I arrived at the restaurant across from the lot. Since it was well past closing, I didn't have to slip the manager anything which meant I saved the firm a buck or two. That goodwill might help before all the doings had been done. I couldn't help but notice a couple of other cars parked down the block, which might not be unusual but did give me some pause. I thought it may be that the feds had a little problem of their own when it came to corruption.

I called Thompson. "I think there are some guys here that ain't feds and ain't locals. Maybe they're gonna go in and see if Mr Garson is home and will do so sooner rather than later."

"Starkey said the same thing," Thompson said. "I've already called Donovan, but you stay out of it, unless you fear for the life of Garson."

Before I could answer, I saw a big van pull up and double park. At this time of night it didn't matter, but it also sent a shiver up my spine. Whoever was in the van was there for no good, and wanted to get out of here in a hurry after they'd finished their no good.

The back door of the van opened and out came four guys dressed totally in black and carrying semiautomatic rifles. The two cars that had worried me proved to be equal to that worry. Both emptied two men and thus there were eight men headed towards the yacht. I didn't think it was the feds, but I wasn't dopey enough to call out a question asking their origin or their religious status. The guys swarmed the decks and went about the business of looking over the yacht, from stem to stern, smashing doors as necessary, to do their business.

As suddenly as the van had rolled up, two large Humvees appeared and parked at opposite ends of the street, effectively sealing off the roads. The driver of the van evidently saw it too, as the van horn immediately began to blast. The eight men who'd run onto the yacht suddenly appeared back on the deck.

A loud speaker rang out through the quiet of the night, "This is the Federal Bureau of Investigation. Please disembark and lay your arms down. Lay on the ground. You will not be injured."

The men seemed to be discussing whethers and whats and then they decided to hit the water. All of them jumping across various points of the ocean. Just as they were hitting the water, two large boats turned their lights on and shined them into the water. The boats came running into where the yacht was located.

The driver of the van cranked his engine and drove towards where the Humvee was blocking the road. I know crazy when I see it and this was crazy. There were about thirty guys out with weapons, that I could see which meant there were likely sixty total, and they opened fire on the advancing van. It came to an abrupt halt well before reaching the Humvee.

Men ran towards the van with their faces covered, suited totally in black, holding weapons with night vision sights. Men that I wouldn't want to meet in brightest sunshine, much less at dark. The door to the van opened and a man extended his arms out and then cautiously exited. As quick as he got out of the van he hit the ground, splayed with his arms outstretched. He definitely did not want those semiautomatics to go off again.

For a gun battle, there hadn't been much to it. I could see the police boats rounding up those who'd jumped in the water. There were a lot of men surrounding the docks and if anyone tried to come out of the water they'd be caught. All in all an effective trap and one that I'd likely set up without knowing. I didn't know whether to be proud that my tax dollars were at work, or mad because I'd been used.

A man with a large gun approached my vehicle and gestured for me to get out. I got out, doing exactly what the van driver had done, extending my arms first and then splaying on the ground.

Several other men came up and surrounded me. One of them got down on one knee and began to frisk me. I let him, keeping my mouth shut. I'd be alright in the end, even if they took me in. The man found my pistol and my ID. Once he saw that I worked for National he said, "Sorry, didn't know you were one of the good guys. We thought only bad guys would be here tonight."

"Just trying to be of help," I lied.

The man returned my gun and ID. I was putting them away when a figure approached, and it looked like Donovan. "Didn't expect to see you here," he said. "But I guess it's understandable. Wanted to see us take down Garson?"

"Did you?" I asked.

"No," he replied. "He wasn't on board when we had a much less pronounced raid earlier today. However, we did enlist the help of the police for a raid we planned at 3 a.m."

"So, someone there leaked it to United Transhipment and they decided to beat you to the prey," I said. "Then you grab the thugs when they come in to get a guy that you know is not there. Not bad. Remind me not to play poker with you."

Donovan laughed, he was likely feeling alright. Even though he didn't have Garson he had a lot of bad guys on weapons and attempted assault, and breaking and entering, and who knew what other charges. Those guys would be willing to trade the fat cats at United Transhipment and that had been the prey of the feds all along.

"I assume the same thing happened at the houseboat slip," I said.

"You assume right," Donovan said. "We've got fifteen bad guys between the two locations. We also got a cop named Paul McNabb as the guy that provided them the information. We had a wireless tap set up and found a burner phone number going out to a guy named Nebo at United Transhipment. We immediately searched every cop at the station and we found Mr McNabb in possession of that burner phone. We have hopes for his cooperation, and big hopes. The last place a cop wants to find himself is in the joint with the guys he put there. I figure this McNabb will sell his soul for a placement in a nice safe federal prison."

"I expect you're right," I said. "You through with me? I've had like zero sleep in the past few days. I'd kinda like to hit the sack."

"We are not only through with you," Donovan replied, "we are thankful to you and will name you in our thank you letter to National for the cooperation of your firm. This was one good day and we want others to bask in the joy of it."

"Thanks," I said. "And I'm sure it will be a feather in my cap and useful during my evaluation." Then I went off to find Bug.

GARSON AT LAST

I called Bug and he growled, as he usually does when he goes a couple of days without booze and without sleep.

"You better not have me out here on a wild goose chase," he said.

"You take your chances, same as I do. The feds have pulled their raid early. It seemed to go well but they didn't find Garson."

"I reckon not," Bug said. "You gonna come relieve me?"

"No. I'm headed to the savings and loan. Just in case they backdoored you."

"Gonna be a long night," Bug growled and hung up the phone.

I got to the Dartmore Savings and Loan about 3 a.m. If they had backdoored Bug and had come here already, likely Garson was long gone. Still, there was an all-points out on him and several police agencies had his picture, so I thought he might still go to ground somewhere in this burg of ours. He knew that once his relationship with Bautner was discovered, it wouldn't be long before this savings and loan would be investigated.

I parked across the street from the savings and loan and luckily there were a couple of cars on the street already. That helped hide me. Then I got out my night glasses. I didn't have long to wait. I saw a car pull up to the savings and loan and two people get out. One I was sure was Mavis Bautner and the other I would bet was our Mr Garson.

I immediately called Bug. "They backdoored you. Get over here fast."

"On my way," he said and I heard the car engine crank as he hung up.

I'd already taped down the door light button on my car, which is standard practice when you expect to leave a car and don't want the overhead light to come on. I drew my gun as I walked cautiously towards the car that was parked in front of the savings and loan. I made it to the far side of the car and got down on one knee, with my eyes barely over the driver front fender.

It was only a couple of minutes, though it seemed like an eternity, before the savings and loan door opened and the lady and gentleman came out with the man carrying a briefcase. I waited until they were about five feet from me before I stood up, and as I stood I cursed Bug for being so damned slow.

"Mr Garson and Ms Bautner," I said. "Kindly drop to the pavement or I'll blast the hell out of you."

Sheer fear ran through their faces, but Garson was nothing if not a survivor. He grabbed the woman with his free hand making her his shield, and dropping his briefcase reached for what I assumed was his gun.

I shot at their legs and really didn't care which one I hit at the time, even though I knew it ain't all that wise to shoot the daughters of rich men. Luck was with me, however, and I heard a man's scream and as Garson hit the ground the lady went down too, shivering. I guess she thought chivalry was dead. I guess she was right.

Just as I walked up and put my foot on the case, a car pulled into the parking lot. Bug, late, but better late than not at all. This was a two-man job—one to cover the bad guys, one to call the cops.

I kicked away the gun that Garson had dropped when I shot him. I didn't want to touch it but I had to do something to get it away from Garson or Bautner for that matter. You never know what crazy things people will do and it's best not to put temptation in their way when they're under stress.

"Call Gonzo, Thompson, the cops and an ambulance," I shouted at Bug, "And in that order."

"Okay," Bug replied, "least you didn't shoot the girl."

The girl, who was not looking any too good was about two seconds from passing out. I said, "You can stand, Mavis, but no nonsense."

She stood shakily. If she was looking for a helping hand, she could keep on looking. Her face was ashen and I thought she was just coming to the realisation that her boyfriend had tried to keep her between him and a bullet. I don't think she liked the idea.

"Damn you!" she shouted and then stomped on his shot leg.

"Stop that," I growled. "You're gonna do something your daddy's money can't get you out of. Now stand there and be quiet. The cops will be here shortly."

And they were. As well as Gonzo and Thompson and an ambulance. Thompson half-laughed when he saw Bug and me and said, "Thought you weren't getting along."

Bug replied, "For fifty thousand dollars I'd even get along with you."

Thompson just laughed. Gonzo eyed us but didn't say anything. Bautner looked blank. Garson was lying on the ground, groaning and holding his leg. The cops rounded us all up and headed everyone but Garson to the station. Garson got an express ride to City Hospital.

THE AFTERMATH

With the testimony of Paul McNabb and Bart Himley, both of whom desired to spend time in a federal pokey instead of the state run institution, Cready got off. McNabb had called Cready and Himley admitted that he and Wreek and Bigg had set up the accident so that their alibi would remain intact.

Sacks owned up to helping the foursome set up the alibi for five thousand, but he claimed he knew nothing about them using the freezer to store Butree. The cops figured he was lying but had him on so many other counts they didn't worry about it.

Wreek hadn't come out of his coma yet and likely would wish he hadn't once he did.

As best the police could piece together, the foursome met Garson at the Night of Colours, just after they'd robbed the bank. Garson took the funds and was supposed to launder the money. Since he was already skimming from his other clients, he had decided to skip and take the $4 million with him.

United Transhipment had brought Starkey in to find Garson, that part was legitimate. However, if Starkey had found Garson then he would have likely wound up dead just like Bigg and Jake.

Bigg and Wreek had visited the Night of Colours to brace Jake on separate nights. Jake was their point of contact with United Transhipment and with Garson. They figured Jake was part of the rip off. He wasn't but United Transhipment figured that if the robbers kept coming around and bugging Jake, then it was just a matter of time before the cops figured out the connection. That was why Jake killed Big and got killed himself trying to take out Wreek.

In the daylight hours, just before the raid, someone had called Mavis Bautner and told her that the raids were going to happen. Mavis didn't know who'd done it, and the cops never proved it was Bug or me, though they tried. Mavis collected Garson from the yacht and the two of them hid out waiting to go to the savings and loan to get the $4 million.

Luckily Bug had the night off, and on his own he had decided to shadow Mavis and he saw her with Garson. He had tried to trail them but they had shaken his tail. They both denied this when questioned but it was immaterial since the cops couldn't prove otherwise.

I happened to call Bug to let him know the raids were over and he told me he had seen them but had lost them while trying to tail them. I thought they may be heading to the savings and loan owned by their father, since Starkey had found a key at Garson's place and it might be the key to a box at a savings and loan. I asked Bug to meet me there, but hadn't called anyone else since I wasn't certain and didn't want to bother others if I was wrong.

The cops didn't like our testimony but that's the version Bug and I decided to go with beforehand and we stuck with it. It's weak, I know, but it was the best we could do.

Regardless of how we came upon the savings and loan, it was there that we found Mavis and Garson. Mavis had a master key since she did a lot of business there with her firm, and her father owned the place. Garson had likely selected the place before he had even contacted Mavis, since he knew her father owned it and that she still carried a torch for him. Regardless of the why, he had stashed the $4 million along with a host of Swiss bank codes in a safety deposit box. They had grabbed it and were off to parts unknown when I stepped in and ruined their game.

Garson went state's evidence and the money laundering firm of United Transhipment had to close business cause so many of the workers went to prison. The feds sent a nice letter to National praising Thompson, Starkey, Bug and me, and that letter likely went right into the trash bin.

Thompson growled a bit but not anymore than he usually does, so I guess he either forgave us or understood why we did it. Bug and I did get the fifty thousand apiece for the reward. Starkey got mad, but since he was on the Garson case to start with he couldn't get any reward money. National, as I understood it, got an additional quarter of a million from whoever owned First National, or the insurance company that owed the money to First National. I never knew which exactly and I never cared.

Bug and I both wasted the fifty thousand we got, but that's what we always do with money, and we'll both die broke, but with memories of having spent the fifty big ones.

We never talked much about the case after it was over, though I heard that Mavis got off with probation, which goes to show you that money talks and always will. Bug did say one last thing before we went out and debauched ourselves.

"You know, if those bozos hadn't tried to set up an alibi, we would never have caught them. That's what they call poetic justice."

"Maybe," I replied. "But they had to do something, because sometimes even a dead man needs an alibi."

THE END

Wilson Toney was born in 1952 and was raised on a farm. Being a lazy person, he found that the farm life was too much work for too little remuneration, so he became a registered engineer. For close to fifty years he plied his trade and as a result visited 48 of the 50 states and at least fifteen different countries. After retiring, Wilson took up writing. His first work of note is *Alibi for a Dead Man*. Wilson has published two technical books under another name and a movie adaptation for an independent film. Wilson has been married for over forty years to the only woman that would put up with him. His only claim to fame is that he used to live across the way from a man who married a lady that was hit by a meteorite (and yes, that's a true story).

Follow the previous capers of Al Wheeler from the irrepressible...

Carter Brown

The Wench is Wicked / Blonde Verdict / Delilah Was Deadly
978-1-944520-33-5 $19.95
"All fans of crime fiction should take this opportunity to rediscover Brown and Al Wheeler, and experience what kind of stories kept readers happily turning pages when paperback originals first ruled the market."
—Alan Cranis, *Bookgasm*. Al Wheeler #1-3.

No Harp for My Angel / Booty for a Babe / Eve, It's Extortion
978-1-944520-44-1 $19.95
"These three novels are testaments to Brown's authorial leanness... With succulent descriptions of succulent women, two-fisted action, twists and turns, and Wheeler's irrepressible attitude, there's nothing *not* to like in Brown's series about this rakish police officer."
—Kristofer Upjohn, *Noir Journal*. Al Wheeler #4-6.

No Law Against Angels / Doll for the Big House / Chorine Makes a Killing
978-1-944520-70-0 $19.95
"...a gripping short read...Al Wheeler is hilarious with his endless sarcasm, never completely in control but somehow being three steps in front of the bad guys and the reader. This is absolutely entertaining and a must read."
—*Paperback Warrior*

"A mix of sex, violence, mystery, and police procedural all wrapped in a pure pulp bundle."
—*Just a Guy That Likes to Read*

Stark House Press, 1315 H Street, Eureka, CA 95501
griffinskye3@sbcglobal.net/www.StarkHousePress.com
Available from your local bookstore, or order direct or via our website.

Lightning Source UK Ltd.
Milton Keynes UK
UKHW020642101219
355109UK00012B/685/P